passages

Tim—
Hope you enjoy the journey ☺

passages

WILTED LILY Series
— Book Two —

Kelli Owen

Gypsy Press

For Frank Errington, I think you would have approved of this incarnation.

Acknowledgments: Thanks to Amanda Fidler for beating on the super rough and babysitting series continuity. To Bob Ford for once again helping my Midwest appropriately sound Southern hick. To my red pens of doom: Tod Clark and Ron Dickie. To the believers and nonbelievers alike. And to the con-goers and Lily lovers who requested to be in her next story, here you go—you may or may not last through the series. I make no promises.

Walking with a friend in the dark is better than walking alone in the light.

~ Helen Keller

The iron gates hung open and broke the tree line along the road like the great gaping mouth of some unseen monster. As the car slowed down, the gentle clicking of the blinker filled the silence, and Lily May's heart skipped a beat. The maroon sedan turned and passed a small stone building with an oxidized copper plaque declaring they had arrived at McMillan School for Boys. If Lily May hadn't spent the better part of the ride listening to the calming thoughts of the man who had been here before, the maw of iron and the lichen covered gatehouse would have been intimidating. Instead, she found herself sitting up taller in the back seat, vying for a better look at her new home.

The drive had taken all night and the better part of the morning. Having never left Sussex County before, Lily May was mildly disappointed the scenery had been cloaked in darkness for most of the trip. The moonless night and gentle hum of the engine had lulled her to sleep about the same time the thoughts of the men escorting her had begun to wander aimlessly and provide no more details.

Until then, their minds had been a cornucopia of information.

The two men in the front seat, wearing suits like required uniforms rather than tailor-made decisions, thought of everyday things—their wives and children, their paychecks, and the boat one of them hoped to finally have enough to purchase. The man with the shiny cowboy boots, who had introduced himself as Mr. Erne, sat in the back seat with Lily. He was *not* government, as the detective had thought, and was as eager to hear her talk, as she was to listen to his *inner* voice and the secrets he might hold.

Mr. Erne had spoken with Lily May's mamma and meemaw for over an hour in their humble living room, enjoying stale cookies and fresh iced tea, while discussing Lily May's *abilities*. He had heard her outlandish testimony regarding her kidnapping and rescue. And he had believed *every single word* the young girl had blurted, mumbled, or otherwise shared. His desire was to help her learn to both control *and* freely use her abilities, at what he referred to as an *educational playground for gifted children*. Lily May heard his thoughts and knew he truly believed it was a good place, good enough to trust with his own family members.

Sussex County had been afraid of Lily May since she was little, and the three adults discussing her life soon agreed it was best for her to leave fear behind, even if it meant leaving family. He handed her mamma a thick envelope and a folded piece of glossy paper, promising they could visit whenever they wished.

She packed the only important possessions she could think of in a tiny brown battered suitcase borrowed from her mamma—a suitcase she'd only ever seen in her parents' room, but never witnessed being used. Even though Mr. Erne claimed they would provide clothing and toiletries, Lily May packed a handful of outfits, including her favorite summer dress and the matching pajamas she had made in stitching class. She grabbed the cracked, framed picture of her parents—taken long before her birth at someone's backyard barbeque—and placed it on her folded clothes, before covering it with the thin quilt her meemaw had made for her. She looked around her small room at the things she was leaving behind. She palmed her beat up Bible—a present from Pastor Jacob when she'd gradated from Sunday school to regular church in seventh grade—and added it to the suitcase before closing it. She hugged Mamma and Meemaw, twice each, through tears of hopeful anxiety, and waved good-bye to the only home she'd ever known.

The first leg of the journey was filled with

questions and answers—*some* spoken. Mr. Erne asked, Lily May answered, and then Lily May often heard his internal reactions. He wasn't afraid of her, which felt both foreign and wonderful to Lily May. He was pleasant and seemed nice, but he had a sadness to him that had softened, like aged pain you've grown accustomed to. She heard his thoughts of missing his wife, Bree— lost while giving birth to their daughter. He was sad. But he so *absolutely* adored his daughter— making her his number one priority—even his sad thoughts were washed with happiness. She almost immediately, instinctively, trusted him.

Tommy wasn't convinced yet.

Tommy had sat unseen by Mr. Erne throughout the drive. He alternated between a crouched position on the center hump of the backseat floor and boldly sitting between them, as if providing a barrier for Lily May against the man. Lily May was pleased Mr. Erne fully believed in Tommy, even though the man couldn't see her young ghostly companion. Mr. Erne had even asked if Tommy would be joining them when they stopped for dinner.

"Mister," Lily May giggle-snorted and shook her head. "He don't eat nothing no more."

"He's still welcome to sit with us." Lily heard the unspoken rest of the sentence, clear as day. *I'm sure he stays close anyway.*

"Actually, he used to like to wander 'round

like a little adventurer—calls himself Huck Finn, 'cos I had to read it for school last year, so I did out loud to him. He would tell me tales of what he'd seen while we were apart." Her smile beamed. It was the first time in her life she'd showed off her talents for hearing thoughts without worrying about the repercussions of fear, hate, or shame.

Mr. Erne nodded and grinned back, his mind suddenly full of names and the notion *they* would all adore her.

"Who are *they*?" She questioned, as she reached down to fetch the shoes she'd kicked off before they'd even pulled off the worn patch of grass Papa referred to as their driveway.

"The other children at McMillan. You'll meet them all soon enough, Little Lady." His smile was kind and reassuring.

"And they're like me?" Lily May wondered how many had died to gain their abilities like Tommy had, and how many were like her—born with it.

"Yes. Maybe? I guess it depends on exactly what all you can do. According to what you told the detective, you can hear the thoughts of the living and communicate with the dead."

"*Communicate* sounds so fancy. I just talk with 'em, and they talk back. I help 'em talk to family if that's what they want." Lily May shrugged. "The living though? That's usually just hearing turmoil or excitement. Like if they're emotional or something. *Regular* stuff is like little whispers tickling behind my ears, so I can *almost* tune them out completely to make the world quiet. But if I *wanna* hear all the boring stuff, I gotta try harder and let my inside get real quiet. Them emotional things though? I can't almost ever stop them. That's as good as screaming it right at me."

He sat back in his seat. Lily May recognized his expression as what Papa called *chewing on them words*.

They ate at a small diner on the side of a busy stretch of road, Tommy sitting on the foot rail under the counter watching them. Lily May meticulously pulled the crust from her grilled cheese before devouring it, repeatedly dipping the edge into a spot of ketchup meant for her French fries. Under the bright lights of the diner booth, Lily May noticed Mr. Erne's hair was almost the same color as his cream shirt, but the honey and silver in his mustache and goatee told her it was dyed to cover those gray hairs. She declined dessert, not wanting to be a bother or take advantage, but Mr. Erne had ordered some to go. Back in the car, with a piece of rhubarb pie in a Styrofoam box, they headed into the darkness of night, and the minds around her quieted.

Lily May awoke some time after the sun had

risen, when they left the steady hum of concrete and blacktop for the curves and bumps of less maintained backroads. The woods appeared thick at first glance, but when she squinted, she realized it was only a barrier, nothing more than a thick strip of evergreens and oaks. As the sun rose higher and illuminated the thin spots, fields, occasional farmhouses, and other buildings could be seen hiding behind the canopy.

Home.

Lily May heard Mr. Erne's thought and turned to see an expression of relief on his face, as if he'd missed the building itself.

He met her gaze as they drove through the gate. "Welcome to McMillan Hall."

"But the plaque?" Lily May held her thumb out to indicate the little stone gatehouse behind them, which had said *School for Boys*.

"Ah yes, originally it *was* a school for boys, but things have changed. We just call it a hall now. You'll learn that and much more once we get you settled."

The trees opened up and Lily May saw in person the grounds and building she'd only previously pulled from Mr. Erne's mind. The driveway led to a large circular roundabout, the inside boasting lush grass and several flowering bushes with a tall gray statue on a white pedestal standing above it all at the center.

"Mrs. McMillan herself." Mr. Erne provided as he pointed toward the statue, his eyes wandering across the building rather than focusing on the statue.

"Missus?" Lily May hadn't even considered the school could be named for a woman, but Mr. Erne either didn't hear her question or was too busy in the myriad of thoughts running through his mind. She squinted at the statue and saw it was indeed a woman, wearing a two-piece skirt and jacket like in the old movies, a small hat on her head, and her hands folded demurely in front of her against the folds of her skirt.

Looking away from the statue to the grounds around it, Lily May's gaze followed a narrow road as it branched off the roundabout to the right. She saw it forked near the corner of the hall, one tine continuing toward a smaller building set further back in the expansive, neatly trimmed grounds, the other disappearing around the side of the building, presumably wrapping around to the back. The car came to a stop in front of the building. Straight ahead, left of the main building, Lily May could see the entrance for a parking area, which broke free of the roundabout and currently held a handful of vehicles, including two large, white, passenger vans with navy lettering on the side simply stating McMillan.

Engrossed in her surroundings, she hadn't

heard Mr. Erne exit the car or the quiet click of the trunk latch being released. The slamming of metal behind her made her jump and she turned to see Mr. Erne, with her suitcase in his hand, opening the door for her.

Lily May stepped out and looked past Mr. Erne to the building itself, her head tilting further and further back as her gaze continued upward. A set of wide stone stairs led from the roundabout to the richly colored wood of the massive front doors. The stone building spread out from its entrance, depositing windows along the arms, which stretched a hundred feet in either direction and rose up two taller than normal stories. A third story sat only above the center of the building, graced with an oversized clock stopped at two forty-five. She didn't know if it had broken during the day or the middle of the night, but Lily May knew the time was wrong, as the sun hadn't yet passed noon in the sky.

The door shut behind her and the car drove off, bypassing the parking lot to continue out to the main road and disappear. Lily May realized the men in the front seat were escort only and understood why their thoughts hadn't provided anything about the school. In the car's absence, there were no city sounds, or noises from a busy road. The grounds were silent, except for the chattering of squirrels and songbirds.

Off the beaten path, erected somewhere deep in the countryside of northern Pennsylvania, McMillan Hall was a hulking stone monument to peace of mind.

Or so Lily May hoped.

— t · w · o —

Lily May sat on what looked like an out-of-place church pew in an alcove off the main hallway. There were three different doors around her, but Mr. Erne had given her the suitcase and disappeared into the one across the way. She put her suitcase on the floor and sat on the bench, wiggling her toes and wishing she could take her shoes off. It had been a long ride and her feet felt cramped. Concern grabbed hold of her when she realized she usually only wore shoes when out in public, to the store or school, but now she lived in the school, and she worried she'd never be barefoot again. Her jaw ached and she remembered the bruise there and the things she'd been through. The kidnapping she'd barely survived.

Shoes are the least of my troubles.

Her hand went to her sore face, but she tried to take her mind off it and the shoes by surveying her surroundings and trying to get a feel for the place she'd agreed to live.

When they had entered the building, Mr. Erne had walked her right past two sets of wide, majestic stairs—leading up *and* down on her left, but up only on her right. Beyond them, Mr. Erne stopped at an intersection of hallways, the hub of the building. In front of them she saw a set of doors, closed and marked with a brass plaque reading DINING. Left of the doors was a boys' restroom, and beyond it was an alcove with a closed door and unoccupied desk, a wooden nameplate declared it to be the *NURSE*. To the right of dining hall was a girls' restroom, followed by another small alcove with an older black woman sitting at a desk. At their arrival, she looked up and smiled broadly, stood to greet Mr. Erne, and scurried into the doorway to her left. Mr. Erne had directed Lily May to the bench in the larger alcove opposite of them, and then followed the woman into the office without closing the door.

There was something about the school gnawing at Lily May, as she sat in the quiet alcove and listened to her surroundings. It was massive to Lily May, easily the biggest building she'd ever been in, but there was something beyond the size scratching at her curiosity. At each end, the hall turned, and Lily May imagined it continued into opposing wings. Both the exterior and interior of the school appeared very much as Mr. Erne had held in his thoughts, but there was a strange haze to it. It was almost as if there were spots of fog running along the floor and stretching down the walls. She squinted and looked for ghosts, or people, and saw neither.

The exposed wood around her was beautiful, richly colored, and something worthy of the bigger cathedrals she'd only ever seen on television. The floor was a polished, shiny field of beige ceramic tiles with reddish-brown grout between them. Unusual coloring on its own, but next to the richly hued wood of the walls, it blended seamlessly to the aesthetics. A variety of tones and grains, in no particular order or pattern, stretched up the wall from the floor in strips to a high chair rail with intricate yet repetitive carvings along it. The planned randomness reminded Lily of Meemaw's quilts.

Above the rail, light beige paint stretched up toward the twelve-foot ceilings, dappled, as if someone had rolled a rag around in it before the paint had dried. Above her, pale ceiling tiles with an almost indiscernible pattern, were edged by a plain strip of wood the same dark color as the chair rail.

It was beautiful, elegant, and made Lily May feel small and insecure for being *a minute from sixteen* but not knowing any of the proper terms for what she was looking at. She was simple. She came from simple folk. And this felt far too fancy for her comfort. But there was something else. Something deeper. She felt it around her, hanging in the very air. There was something akin to sadness. In the foggy parts of the hallway, the wood looked funny, like there was a shadow on it. She squinted and could almost imagine wallpaper stretching from ceiling to floor, rather than the current beige paint above and wooden boards below.

What was here before?

Mr. Erne came out of the office and approached Lily May. "Miss Mac is going to take care of you, Little Lady. See you in class." Without another word, he headed to her right and disappeared around the corner at the end of the hallway.

The older black woman reappeared from the inner room and glanced at her desk, "Aww, you wonderful man." She spoke to the small Styrofoam box they'd gotten at the diner as she picked it up. Lily May knew it held a piece of pie, but hadn't even seen Mr. Erne carry it in, let alone leave it on the desk.

The woman put the container on the cabinet behind her and looked up at Lily May, "Come on over here, dear." She used her head and one hand to indicate Lily should come her direction. The woman's accent was country.

Not southern, like mine, but not city neither.

Lily May obediently stood, fetching her small

suitcase from the floor, and crossed the tile hallway. The woman was somewhere between Mamma and Meemaw in age, thin but in a healthy way, not like the skinny poor of Sussex County eating government cheese and black and white labeled canned corn. A headful of long black braids framed a pleasant face speckled with what Meemaw always called *beauty spots*. She had soft taupe eyes that sparkled, and Lily May heard her mamma's voice talking about, *people what smile with them eyes*. The woman's frame, hair, and accent immediately reminded Lily May of her classmate's mother back home. A flare of homesick rose in her chest, and for a moment she wondered if she'd made the right decision.

Lily May stopped in front of the woman and a soft hand reached forward to covered her own. The woman immediately looked up at Lily May, her eyes full of sympathy as she swallowed hard over pain that wasn't hers. "Oh, you poor dear."

Lily May would have thought the woman was referring to the visible bruise along her jawline, but her eyes spoke volumes and Lily May knew this woman somehow knew *everything* she'd recently gone through. Lily was glad she wouldn't have to explain the bruises, but expected she'd have to at *some* point.

Miss Mac gave her simple white dress a once-over. "We can get you into some fresh clothes.

That kind of drive is rough on even your Sunday best."

"Yes, Miss Mac?" A light, youthful voice behind Lily May made her flinch. She spun toward the sound, pulling her hand away in the process.

"You precious thing." Miss Mac crinkled her nose at the young blonde girl. Lily May noted the other girl's hair was like honey, a softer blonde, and not the stark *yellow-white* of her own. Miss Mac continued, smiling at the girl while holding a hand out to indicate Lily May. "*This* is Lily May, your new roommate. Would you be a doll and show her on upstairs to your room?"

"Yes, Miss Mac." The other girl nodded and seemed eager to please the woman.

"Thank you so much, Little Miss Precious."

The girl blushed and spun to Lily May, sticking out her hand. "I'm Caroline. Our rooms are this way. Follow me."

Lily May reached forward to shake the girl's hand, but Caroline dodged the gesture and moved instead for Lily May's suitcase. The girl stopped, leaning to look behind Lily May for a moment, her brows furrowing as she resumed her attempt to grab Lily's luggage. Lily May's grip tightened on the only possessions she had in the world.

The girl stood up, acknowledging Lily May wasn't giving up the suitcase, "Okay... and um."

PASSAGES

She shrugged and shook her head, "Never mind. This way." Caroline turned and led Lily May back toward the front door, pivoted at the stairs, and headed up the wide set of wooden stairs.

Lily followed her, noting a black patch on each step meant for either grip or noise reduction, or both. The girl's gait had a light spring to it, *almost* like she was skipping but not quite. She wore flowered capris and a yellow top, her long honey-blonde hair hanging straight down her back and bouncing along with her cadence. An occasional squeak from her small white sneakers rang out through the halls. A part of Lily had expected uniforms, so she was surprised there didn't seem to be one.

Then again, it's all but summer. Are they more casual during the break? Do they get a summer break? She regretted not asking Mr. Erne what the actual school year was.

At the mid-landing the girl turned back and studied Lily May, eyebrows raised with an expression of curiosity. The girl leaned to the side, peering behind Lily for a long moment as her eyes narrowed.

"Who's the boy?" Caroline stood upright and folded her hands in front of her chest like a parent waiting for an admission of guilt.

Lily May turned and glanced down the stairs, expecting a student she didn't know. She saw no one but Tommy and turned back to the girl, shrugging.

"Him. Can you see him?" Caroline pointed directly at Tommy, and he stared at her with an open mouth.

"Who, *Tommy*?" Lily May looked between Tommy and Caroline, unsure how to feel about someone else being able to see him.

"Red shirt? Sixish? Yeah. Him. Is he nice or mean?"

"Mean?" Lily May couldn't fathom the notion. "He's nice. And he's *almost* seven, but he's just little, so you be nice to him!" She stood tall, in a protective stance, and Caroline put her hands up in surrender.

"No worries. He *looks* nice, I was just checking." She smiled at Lily May, then leaned around her and smiled at the ghost on the stairs. "Tommy is it?"

He nodded frantically and whispered, "Lily May, she can *see* me."

Caroline turned back to the stairs and continued upward, giggling, "Of course I can, silly. But you're going to freak Miko right out." She made her way to the second floor with a spring in her step.

"Okay then, here's your super quick tour." Caroline turned out of the stairwell and moved toward a large T-section of hallway, an intersection like the first floor. "This is the second floor foyer. From here you can go to the dorms, the suites, the bathrooms or the library." She pointed to the doors immediately to the left, then the right. "Male teacher suites are on that side. Female on this side." Waving at the left again, as if it didn't matter, she said, "Around the corner, that's West Wing over there. We're East. This way." She turned to her right. "Oh, and the Library of course." She pointed at the oversized, ornately carved door directly across from the stairs, just as it opened and a young girl exited.

Lily May peered beyond the student at the rows and stacks. The girl leaving the library pushed past her, bumping into her hard enough to almost knock her suitcase free.

"Watch where you're going." The girl scrutinized Lily May up and down with a curled lip snarl. Her arched eyebrows were plucked so thin Lily May thought they were almost gone. Her dark hair was cut in a short jagged bob poking out every which way, and Lily wasn't sure if it was naturally wild or by design. "So? What are you?" She spat her question at Lily May. Lily baulked, the girl's voice matching her angry appearance. "You a push… or a *pull*?"

"This way, Lily May." Caroline grabbed Lily's arm and tore her away from the other girl's attention, quickly leading her to the right wing. "This bathroom and showers is for the boys. Ours are back on the other side of the Library." She spoke as they passed the closed, clearly marked door. Opposite the bathroom door, the wall opened into a short offshoot hallway leading to three doors—suites for the female teachers as Caroline had pointed out—and Lily imagined the male side was similar.

"Who was that? What did she mean? A pusher?" Lily May glanced back toward the girl but followed Caroline forward. "I'm both, like you." She remembered Caroline talking to Tommy. "I can speak to *and* hear from."

Caroline stopped and turned toward Lily May. "That's not what that means here." She seemed to pale a little before turning back around and continuing.

At the corner, Caroline pointed to the open door. "That's the lounge where we all hang out at night." She turned left at the corner of the hallway, took several steps, and opened the first door on the right. "And *this* is us." She stepped in and flicked a light switch on the wall. An overhead light housed in an ancient glass dome came to life.

"What was that about? What did she me—?" Lily May followed Caroline into the room and stopped.

The room was bigger than Mamma's living room and much bigger than any room Lily May had ever seen shared among siblings. Split down the middle like a dorm room, each side sported a small closet on the wall nearest the door, followed by a dresser, a bed, and matching desks under the two windows. The desk and dresser on the right side of the room were adorned with books, folded papers, a jewelry box, ponytail holders and other signs of life. Hanging off the post of the unmade bed, a backpack as battered looking as Lily May's own suitcase hung as if forgotten.

"You get this side. We'll go get you some bedding." Caroline pointed to the bare mattress bookended by an empty dresser and desk.

"Is everyone's room this big?" Lily May spun around, inspecting the space. She paused at the closet and gasped. There were more empty hangers in the closet than all the clothes she had *ever* owned.

"Yeah, well, most. Some are bigger."

Lily May turned to face Caroline, *bigger,* she thought. She set her suitcase on the floor next to the bed and promptly remembered the girl by the library.

"Who was that in the foyer?"

Caroline sighed. "I suppose... better to be warned. *That* was Alyssa. And yes, it's pronounced like that—ah-leeease-ah, a whole lotta long Es. If you try and say Ah-lis-uh, she'll likely swing at you, and it looks like you been swung at enough."

Lily May's hand went up to her jawline and

she waited, but Caroline continued on about the girl in the hall rather than question the one in front of her.

"She tries to be mean and tough, but I think she's just really pissy because she never had anything personalized as a kid. You know how easy it is to find Caroline on a keychain? Not Alyssa though... She's a senior, though. She'll graduate soon enough and we'll be free of her attitude."

Lily May nodded, noting a hostile student she planned to avoid. "And push and pull? You said it was different here? I mean, everything is different here, but how'd you mean?"

"Yes, it's different. And yes, you were half right. You *are* a puller. I'm a puller. Everyone on our side is a puller. The pushers are all in the West Wing, though I don't think there are very many over there right now. Hard to tell. They keep us apart." Caroline's speech sped up a little, as if she were trying to rush through the explanation to get to something else. "Think of it like this. *Pullers* are able to pull information, whether it's through speaking or touching or whatever. They pull knowledge *toward* them. Pushers are..." Caroline's voice trailed off and she swallowed before stepping back out into the hall. "Here, let me show you down to the back stairs."

"Back stairs? Okay." Lily May squinted her

eyes and tried to hear Caroline's thoughts. She got nothing for her effort and joined the girl in the corridor. Several doors opened and closed, and other teens meandered past them, heading back toward the foyer, library, and main stairs. There were many thoughts being thrown into the air around Lily May.

So many of them. And all of them thinking so loudly.

If covering her ears would have helped, Lily might have done so. Instead she heard about homework and boys and fights with parents. This one was happy and that one nervous about a test she didn't study for. And that one—

Wait… Was that a ghost?

Lily May squinted at a light-haired boy who waved at Caroline. She was going to dismiss it because of the gesture, but remembered Caroline could see Tommy, too. There was a tickle to the thoughts in the hall, like when she could hear the dead, and she was about to ask Caroline who the ghost was, but another boy slapped his shoulder and looked directly at Lily May with a wickedly confident smile.

"Hey, a new girl." His short black hair was spikey, standing straight up on his head in places, and his eyes were full of mischief.

"Hi, Alex." Caroline smiled at the light-haired boy, but shook her head at the other. "Go to class, Sam."

Lily May watched the youthful crowd move on and the hallway returned to empty. They had been a mix of girls and boys, short and tall, all seemingly high school age like Lily May. And Tommy—

Lily May looked around and saw him sitting against the wall in the corner by the lounge door, eyes wide.

Tommy? Are you okay?

He nodded and spoke to her with only his thoughts. *That was a lot of... things.*

Lily May furrowed her brows at him.

He waved at her with both hands. *I'm okay. You go with her. I'll wait here.*

She turned back to Caroline to find the girl's eyebrows so high they were almost lost in her bangs. It took Lily a moment to realize what the problem was. Caroline could hear and talk to ghosts, but only out loud. When Lily May and Tommy spoke with their inner voices, Caroline couldn't hear it. *Huh,* Lily thought as she smiled at Caroline. "You said sumthin' about back steps?"

Caroline glanced at Lily May, then back at Tommy and squinted one eye. "You guys talk without talking, don't ya?" She considered them both again and then nodded to herself before Lily could bother to answer.

Caroline turned and headed down the long corridor. "Nothing but dorms down here, bedrooms for the students. All of them are occupied but not everyone has a roommate right now."

Lily May caught up to Caroline and walked next to her rather than behind her. As Lily scanned the empty hallway, she noticed each door had a white board hanging on it. Caroline pointed to the door directly across from theirs. "Kaleigh and Odette are in that room."

The names were written in glitter on small, boards hanging above the white board on twisted wires. "Everyone has their name on their door, then underneath we can leave messages for each other. It's basically our version of cellphones, that and the notes slipped under doors."

Caroline smiled and lifted the marker hanging from a length of string. She drew what looked like a cat butt, laughed, then turned back to Lily May. "You'll like Kals, even though she's a red head. Though she'd call it auburn, but it's still red, just dark. Odette is really new, so you two have that in common, but I don't know a whole ton about her yet. She's only been here about a month. She doesn't like to be touched, though, so try and remember that."

Lily May followed Caroline down the hall, as she pointed at names on doors and gave simple summaries of her classmates.

"Miko is kind of afraid of everything, but really, *really* nice. No roommate for her right now. Her roomie left last winter because of a family emergency and never came back. A couple weeks after she left, a tall ugly woman in a boring dress came and gathered all her things without a word."

"What happened to *your* roommate?" Lily May wondered out loud.

"I just moved over to the dorms, uh… I've never had one." She chewed her lip for a minute and watched Lily May, studying her.

Lily May could tell she was thinking something, but realized she still couldn't hear the girl's thoughts and the surprise must have shown on her face.

"What?"

"I can't hear your thoughts. Even if I try."

"And?" Caroline raised an eyebrow at her. "Wait, do you *always* hear thoughts? Of *everyone*?" Her eyes widened as Lily May nodded sheepishly. *"Thaaaat's* gotta suck." Caroline drew out the word, her inflection one of sympathy rather than teasing.

Lily May laughed, it wasn't the response she was used to, or expecting.

"I thought you just played with ghosts, but that's cool too. I mean… maybe. Wait, you can't hear mine?"

Lily May shook her head with a subtle shrug, and Caroline pinched her lips together in thought. "We'll come back to that! Meanwhile,"

She pointed at the door next to theirs. "CJ is Sam's older sister, the boy earlier with the dark hair? She—serious as a heart attack—looks just like him. And she's okay I guess, but she's a senior. They have different class schedules and they basically ignore us. Her roomie Penny is nice, if not a little odd. I think she sees things."

Caroline shrugged and continued.

"And the one after that is Alyssa and Tasha. Tasha is about as nice as Alyssa is mean. She's awesome to go to in a pinch if you're upset, too. She can just touch you and calm you down. It's like magic."

Caroline raised her hands and moved them around, as if doing some sort of magic trick, then spread them out in front of her to indicate something Lily May wasn't seeing.

"And then we enter The Cave. The boys' end." She covered her mouth and widened her eyes like she was sharing a secret. "First up, the seniors."

She pointed at doors faster now, as she walked toward the end.

"Judd, no roommate. No idea why. Really quiet and keeps to himself. Preston and Drake. Preston is really cute but completely clueless of any of girls. Drake *wishes* he had that problem. And then back down to the juniors and our level. Shane and Keagan. A ginger and a sports nut."

"Who's his favorite driver?" Lily May

questioned, remembering Papa's love of all things NASCAR.

"Driver? Like *car* racing?" Caroline blinked quickly several times and shook her head. "No, no. Football, baseball, basketball. Heck, I think he's even into soccer. But not hockey. He's got some weird thing against hockey. Something about his state being the coldest but not having a *damn* hockey team?"

"His state?" Lily May hadn't even considered they had come from all corners of the country. For whatever reason, she'd thought they were all local.

"Wisconsin, I think. Or Minnesota, maybe? Which one doesn't have a professional hockey team?"

Lily May shrugged, Papa never watched hockey. No one she knew did.

"Doesn't matter. It's *sci-fi cold* according to him and nowhere I would ever visit."

Caroline smiled and turned to indicate the last door on the left. "Sam and Alex from before. Goofballs, but I adore them both. And over here," she turned to the last door on the right, "is Carlos. He's our T.A and lead dorm monkey. He's the senior given the big room at the end and supposed to keep us off the back stairs." She pointed to the stairs beyond Sam and Alex's room.

"T.A.?" Lily May looked at Carlos' door, hoping for an explanation.

"Oh, Teacher's Assistant. Carlos is super nice and really, *really* caring. He's a good leader for us dorm monkeys." She turned back down the hall. "And that's all of us. We should head to class, we're late for…" She paused for a beat. "Science class."

"It's really a school?"

"Sure. Sort of… Mostly." Caroline headed toward their room, again almost skipping as she went, this time with the addition of light humming, repeating the bars as if a tune were stuck in her head.

Lily May could barely see the shadow of Tommy at the other end, by their room door. Between them, another boy suddenly walked across the hall. He didn't speak. He didn't look at them. And he didn't open or close any doors. He simply came from the left wall and disappeared into the right where there was no doorway.

"Is Tommy the only ghost in here?" Lily May could feel the tickle of several dead voices, but couldn't quite make out what they were saying and wondered if they were somewhere else in the building.

"You saw that, too?" Caroline looked back at her.

Lily May nodded.

Caroline turned and kept walking. "Tommy's the only one with a name."

— t·h·r·e·e —

As they reached their bedroom door, Caroline and Lily May were stopped in the hall by a tall woman with glasses and hair the shade of an overripe tomato, obviously dyed.

"Hi, Miz Yost." Caroline hopped through her doorway, grabbed a book and folder from her desk, and was back to the door before the light echo of her words had faded in the otherwise empty hallway. "We're headed to class right now."

"You go on ahead, Caroline. I'm going to be taking our new student down to my office. Let your…" The woman paused, and Lily May watched a flash of something move across Caroline's face. The woman saw it as well, and finished her sentence with inflection. "Tell *Mr. Erne* she's with me."

"*Mr. Erne?* That's our science teacher?" Lily May's eyes brightened at the name.

Caroline looked from Lily May to the woman and back. "Yup, our *science teacher*. See ya later."

She quickly walked past the two of them and disappeared around the corner to the stairs.

"Hello, Lily May. I'm the medical staff here. I'm sorry I wasn't available when you arrived. I was occupied in the West Wing. But if you could come with me, I need to finish processing you before you're let loose in the wild here."

Loose in the wild? Medical staff? Her speech was strange, as if part of something bigger than just the nurse's station Lily May had seen downstairs. And she had at least an opinion if not an attitude toward Lily May's classmates.

"Yes ma'am."

Lily May followed the woman back to the nurse's station and into the small room next to the desk. Closing the door behind them, the woman proceeded to take Lily May's basic measurements—height, weight, blood pressure, and temperature—then grabbed a clipboard from the smaller desk in the room.

Seeing no other staff or other nameplates, Lily May put two and two together and presumed Miz Yost was indeed the nurse.

"And how old were you when you got your first period?" The nurse looked at her clipboard and back up to Lily May before she leaned forward. "You *have* gotten your period, haven't you?"

Lily May's eyes widened and she looked at Tommy, sitting on the edge of a twin sized sick bed, his feet swinging freely above the floor. He shrugged at her horrified look, clearly not understanding the subject matter, and Lily May shooed him from the room with nothing but her expression.

She turned back to the nurse, "Yes, ma'am, I have. I was thirteen. About two and a half years ago." Lily May watched the nurse flip to a different page, read something, and then write several sentences on the front page where she'd previously been marking notes.

"Ma'am? Can I ask why my monthly is important?" Lily May sat taller, trying to see what the woman was writing.

"Because we're tracking whether age of first period and how heavy or horrible it might be, or puberty in general for that matter, has any connection to your powers."

Lily May blinked and thought about what the nurse had said for a moment, rerunning what she thought it meant.

"My *powers*?"

"Yes. Your *powers*. Just like the rest of them." Lily May saw as much as heard the woman's annoyance.

"The rest? Are you *studying* us here?" Lily May thought back to the detective, remembering his thoughts and fears about the government being involved. "Are you studying us and simply going to *admit* you are?"

This can't be real.

"Actually, yes." The nurse nodded, pen poised above Lily May's file. "Many of the students that come through here can read minds. I find it less hassle in the end to just be honest." *With the little shits,* she thought.

Lily May raised her eyebrow at the nurse's derogatory thought.

"And obviously you're one of them." The nurse smiled at her over her glasses.

Lily May relaxed her worry, as she realized it was simply a test. Likely one of many to come, if Mr. Erne's conversations in the car had been truthful.

"Can you take your dress off? I'd like to check your wounds. Neil's notes say you may have broken ribs?"

Lily May nodded and did as she was told. The room felt cold against her skin and she tried not to think of the cold damp basement where she'd gotten the injuries. The nurse winced when she saw the black and blue around Lily's collarbone, the deep purple and yellows along her ribs.

"Well that's one way to get out of PE. No gym for you for at *least* a couple weeks. I'll let Coach know and check you again before you're approved to participate."

The nurse took off the thin brown elastic bandage the police had hastily wrapped around Lily, and grimaced at the bruising hidden underneath. She asked Lily to take several deep breaths and cough twice, while the woman pressed against the angry purple marks and watched Lily's face. The nurse replaced the brown wrap with a much wider, tighter, white version with Velcro at the end of it. It reminded Lily of a girdle like the one Meemaw wore under her church dresses.

"I can't do x-rays here. We'd have to drive into town. But I don't think it's broken." She poked several spots and lightly pushed on others. Lily flinched but held her composure. "No, I'm going to say they're just bruised. Really horribly bruised, but still just a bruise. Take the wrap off to shower, but put it on again after. And sleep with it. If you can't get it on comfortably or tight enough, come see me, or maybe ask Caroline to help. The tightness will relieve some of the pain. If it doesn't or if it flares up, come see me and I'll give you something to ease the pain and help you sleep."

Lily May nodded and met the nurse's eyes, concentrating on listening to the woman's *inner* voice, but heard nothing.

Strange. Quiet like Caroline had been. But I just heard her call us little...shits. Has she been around the kids long enough to block them? Do they teach that here? Or... does she have powers of her own? Lily hadn't considered the staff being gifted like the children.

"What's on your mind, kiddo?" The nurse leaned forward.

Lily May felt her face scrunch up and knew she didn't have what Papa would call a poker face. She'd have to work on that while in *this* building. "Nothing, Nurse Yost."

"Not *Nurse*, hon, just Miz. I'm not actually a nurse. I was a medic back in the real world. Got myself—" She stopped herself. "Let's just say I needed a change of scenery. I act as the nurse, the medical department as a whole, on the spot doctor if you will, but I'm not a *nurse*. Different degree. Different training. *Miz* Yost works just fine. Now then, let's get through these questions shall we?"

Lily May knew the woman was hiding something, but she didn't get the sense of danger or worry from her. *Let her keep her secrets,* Lily May thought as she nodded and indicated they should continue.

— » · » · « · « —

Twenty minutes later, Lily May found herself back where Mr. Erne had originally left her, directly across from the overly pleasant smile of Miss Mac.

Meemaw would really like her when she visits.

Lily smiled back and settled onto the bench.

Her next stop was a meet and greet with the dean of students, who apparently did double-duty as a counselor of sorts, and—according to Miz Yost—was also in charge of the teaching staff. Miz Yost had been adamant about the dean *not* being her *or* Miss Mac's superior, as the two of them answered *only and directly* to the headmaster. And then Miz Yost had told her about all the *non*-teaching staff Lily May hadn't even seen yet.

It was a lot of names for Lily May to remember—between the staff and the students—and she was glad for brass plaques, desk nameplates, and creatively designed door signs. The three doors around her were marked LOUNGE, DEAN, and HEAD MASTER, and she waited patiently for the center door to open.

Above the pew was a large framed news article, which Lily May hadn't noticed when she had first sat in the alcove. She stood to inspect it further, reading the headline of the 1919 article, the edges of which appeared stained or rather smeared with soot and lightly charred. WIDOW MCMILLAN OPENS PRIVATE BOY SCHOOL FOR WAR ORPHANS.

The picture at the top of the article was the front of the building, taken from the other side of the roundabout so the foreground was an offset shot of the statue in the center of it. The flowering bushes were absent from the manicured circle, and the skeletal remains of scaffolding were still standing near the building itself. On the stone steps stood roughly a dozen people, identified under the picture as the inaugural staff.

The door opened before she'd even begun reading beyond the picture's caption. Lily May turned to see a classy woman with a short professional haircut, a silky blouse the same color as her green eyes, and a tailored business skirt above sensible heels. She looked exactly as Lily May expected her to.

"Lily May? I'm Lori Duran, Mrs. Duran, dean of students. If you could please come in and have a seat." She extended her hand, palm up, and gestured to the open door.

Lily May walked past the woman and entered the room—it smelled as clean as it looked. On the right side, an oversized mahogany desk sat in front of a wall of bookshelves. On a black and leather desk pad were neat stacks of papers, several pens poking out of a short glass cup Lily likened to an unchipped version of Meemaw's prized Depression Glass sugar bowl, and a small silver frame facing away. In front of the desk were two bulky leather chairs, the design matching the one behind the desk, but the style more stationary.

Bookshelves lined the opposite wall as well, the volumes looking old and often referenced, as evidenced by several lying on the shelf near an empty slot. A leather loveseat and round marble side table were butted up to the wall left of the doorway. To the right of the doorway, Lily May saw two stacks of wooden filing cabinets and pondered the secrets and wonders of their contents. In the direct ray of sunshine coming through the large leaded windows, sat a small leafy tree in an antique brass pot. The wood and glass throughout the room shone with the polished gleam of pride and maintenance.

"Please, take a seat by the desk." The woman shut the well-oiled door with little more than a whisper. She moved into her chair and then crossed her hands on the desk in front of her, leaning slightly forward, her lips barely moving into a gesture of friendliness. Lily May found her smile to be subtle, but warm.

"That's a lovely locket." The dean nodded toward Lily, and Lily's hand reflexively went to the tarnished metal hanging from her neck. "Family heirloom?"

Lily shook her head, "Found it at a garage sale when I was little. I really wanted it but didn't have no money. The woman let me brush her dog in trade for it."

"We can probably clean that up for you if you'd like."

"Mamma tried ketchup and cola. Didn't work."

PASSAGES

"Well, if you'll let me, I'll show you a trick with baking soda and toothpaste." The dean's eyes softened.

"She's nice." Tommy whispered to Lily, but she didn't respond. She was watching Mrs. Duran sit perfectly still and calm.

The woman broke the silence. "Lillian May Holloway, you have had quite a time these last few weeks, haven't you?"

"Lily May, *please*. No one's ever actually called me Lillian. No one 'cept..." Lily let her voice fade without finishing the sentence.

"Lily it is." Mrs. Duran ignored the requested addition of her middle name and flipped through a manila folder like the one Detective Travis Butler had at the police department back home. Lily wondered if it was the exact one they had filled with notes and comments and statements after she'd escaped the man who kidnapped her and tried to kill her. The man her Papa's spirit had killed to get her free. "I'm sorry you went through that, and if you'd like, we can provide counseling to help you cope with it. Of course, if *any* of your teachers feel it's necessary, it may become more of a requirement than a choice. For your own health."

"I understand, and thank you. I *think* I'm okay." Lily May began to fidget with her dress, not having had a chance to change yet, she picked at what she believed to be a bit of melted cheese from the previous night's dinner.

"And how's that feel?" Mrs. Duran tapped her own jaw. "Teeth okay? Pain bearable?"

"Seems so. Miz Yost said I should go see her if I need anything."

Mrs. Duran nodded and went back to perusing the file. "Apparently your talents did not *start* during that trauma though. Your whole life?"

"Long as I can remember, yes ma'am."

"And you've been marked as— oh my." The woman's eyebrows went up as she scanned several lines of the report with her finger. "So you're telepathic, but also a medium with strong tendencies toward clair-audience, voyance, and cognition, *plus* aura reading?" She looked up at Lily May, the dean's expression showing she was obviously impressed.

"I don't know what all that means, ma'am." Lily May didn't even think she could spell some of the words she'd heard, let alone define them.

"Understandable. Allow me..." She held a finger up. "First and foremost, you are what they call telepathic, meaning you can hear thoughts. Can you also send your thoughts out to others?"

"Not living people, no. Not since Tommy. He and I could do that before he died. Now I only do that with the dead."

"Tommy? That's the small child whose ghost haunts you?"

Lily May looked at him sitting on the floor by the bookshelves and smiled.

Tommy shot her a goofy face. *I don't haunt you.*

I know that.

Mrs. Duran turned in her chair to follow Lily May's gaze. "You know *what*, dear?"

Lily May's eyes went wide and she looked back to the dean. "You heard that?"

"I did, indeed. I'm also telepathic. Though, only with the living, so I heard only *your* side of that exchange."

"He said he wasn't haunting me." Lily May blushed and looked down to her lap, as if caught doing something wrong. She suddenly realized, knew, and fully appreciated what everyone in her hometown had felt when she crawled inside and pulled out their thoughts.

"I'm sorry to offend you, dear. I won't do it again. In truth, we try *not* to do that here. It's easier to get along if we can all agree to a bit of privacy within our own minds. There are designated times in class when you will practice using your skills, and at those times I ask you open up to others. But otherwise, if you can prevent yourself from hearing others, please do so. And they've all been instructed to do the same."

Lily May nodded and Tommy giggled.

"The other things I listed?" The dean

continued with her explanation, "those were all talents of mediums, those who can communicate with the dead. Some can hear things, that is clairaudience. Some see things, clairvoyance. And others just seem to *know*, and that is claircognizance. You communicate back and forth with them, and can see them, so you're at least two of those. The third is generally seen with it, but not always. We'll look into that further when we work with your skills in class."

"Ma'am?" Lily lifted her hand off her lap but didn't fully raise it when she realized what she was about to do.

"Yes?"

"I *do* know things. I always have. But it ain't with the dead. They gotta talk, with either their inner or outside voice. When I *know* things, it's with the living. Or just about things. And it ain't usually helpful none." Lily stopped, considering whether or not to tell the dean how she could tell when people were going to die.

"So you do have all three? Good. I'll let the teachers know, so they can properly work with you on those." She jotted something down and continued. "And then I see there is a note here with a question mark next to aura reading. Do you see colors around people?"

"Colors? Not that I know of..." Lily May paused and chewed at her lip, she'd have to tell her after all. "But I can see when people are gonna pass. They get all *muddy* looking. Like their colors are smeared. Not colors around them, just the colors *of* them."

"Interesting." Mrs. Duran wrote something down. "And people in your town knew you could do these things?"

Lily May's gaze returned to her dress, this time trying desperately to be lost among the threads. "Yes, ma'am. Shunned me and my family for it. Was hard to make friends. It was real lonely before Tommy."

Lily May heard the woman sigh in understanding. "Well, *that* won't happen here." She shut the folder. "The other students are all gifted with a variety of abilities, and many of the staff are as well."

Lily May looked up and tilted her head, furrowing her eyebrows at the idea of what the dean had proclaimed. "Variety? There are *other* abilities? More than all the things I do?"

"Oh honey..." She again laced her fingers together and leaned forward. "There are many, many, psychic gifts out there. *Talents,* if you will. At any given time there are more than a handful among the students here. Right now we have everything from your type of skills with communication to knowledge-based skills like psychometry or remote viewing. We even have a couple with psionics, suggestion, and telekinesis."

Lily May blinked at her. Those words were even more complicated and confusing than the others.

"Come, I'll give you a proper tour and explain it further, while I tell you a little about the school." She stood and gestured Lily May do the same. Tommy hopped up from his position and the three of them left the office.

Dean Duran pointed out the nurse and reception areas Lily May was already familiar with, and then walked her down the broad hall of the first floor's east wing where the classrooms were in session behind closed doors. She explained a variety of talents, calling them skills and gifts on occasion, and mentioned several times there was nothing and no one aggressive currently housed in the East Wing. Leading her up the back stairs Caroline had previously told Lily May *not* to use, Lily found herself standing in the hallway of dorm rooms once again.

"Mrs. William McMillan built the McMillan School for Boys back in 1919 for families with boys who had lost their fathers in the war. She herself was a wealthy widow with four sons, and not only needed help with them, but had the means to help others like herself. The school functioned as such for many years, as your basic run-of-the-mill private boys' school. In those days, this area was one large room with bunks and trunks, much like their military fathers would have had in their barracks. One night in 1979, a fire broke out in this wing of the building. Most people managed to get out, but the school's reputation was damaged and times were changing, so it was closed and left vacant for over twenty years."

The dean walked about halfway down the hall and stopped, her voice growing softer.

"In 2001, my uncle, Headmaster Landry, opened it back up for girls *and* boys, and changed the *official* name to Hall rather than a School for *Boys*. You see, in the wake of 9/11, psychics around the country were being gathered up, questioned, and harassed regarding the terrorist attacks on the East Coast. There was a need to blame someone, and for a time it appeared it would be people like us. Until Washington was harshly reminded, by several psychics they themselves trust, how they were *indeed* warned of an attack and chose to ignore it.

"The headmaster wanted to provide a safe place for kids with talents, to teach them how to not only use their abilities, but to use them effectively in a career without being shunned or ashamed. The world was changing and he wanted kids like him and his family to have a place in it. He chose this location specifically because of the fire, because two boys died that night. And he thought it would be a good way to *test* those with powers. But it would also be nice for the ghosts to not be alone or feared."

The dean looked up and down the hall.

"This is where they are most active. Often seen going from one side to the other. Sometimes heard by those with the ability, or an open mind. The records for the original school were burned in the fire and the papers refused to print the names of the dead, so we do not know who they are and they have yet to tell us. We only know there are two of them."

There are three, Lily May thought, but decided not to disagree with the woman. Instead she nodded, "I saw one earlier, but it didn't look at me. It was like he was still trapped in his time. I've seen that before. I've tried to help 'em. I can't. It hurts that I can't. They're just *stuck*."

"Depending on which one you saw, yes, he's stuck. When the headmaster bought this building, he thought putting walls and doors and making individual dorm rooms would be enough to disrupt their pattern and break them of their loop. It wasn't. And many students have come and gone over the years and tried. Don't feel bad if you can't help them either."

"How far did the fire go?" Lily thought of the foggy look to the downstairs hallway and the overwhelming notion that there had been wallpaper.

"This wing was burned pretty badly. The

second floor was almost completely rebuilt. Burned beams, boards, and wallpapering was scraped and cleaned, and then steamed to try and get rid of the smell of the fire—which some of our students can still smell. We ended up redoing the tile throughout the downstairs. And the dorm area here? This whole section was rebuilt from the floorboards up. Why?"

"I could *almost* see wallpaper downstairs and I didn't understand. I ain't never seen the ghost of a *place* before. The hall looks funny, *foggy*, with shadows that ain't really there. My whole life I've had questions I couldn't ask without lookin' like a fool, but now…"

"Now you can ask anything. And if I had to guess, I'd say you're seeing the soot and smoke, and interpreting it as shadows and fog. And apparently, the wallpaper, which was really ugly anyway if you ask me."

Lily would have smiled at the dean's joke, but was busy holding back tears, which threatened her composure suddenly.

They ain't gonna shame me or shun me. They gonna accept me, they gonna help *me.*

Any fear she had about the decision to come to the school dissipated with the explanation of unseen fog in the hallways.

Back down the stairs, the dean led Lily May to the closed doors marked DINING. Inside was a massive dining room with over a dozen large tables set in a large U-shape. Stained glass windows on the left and right walls allowed light to flood the room, and a door on each led to the outside—*courtyards with picnic tables*, according to the dean. On the back wall, there were two interior doors at either end, clearly marked IN and OUT. The dean led Lily May through the tables to the back and entered the left door. Inside, the smells of roasted chicken and vegetables hit Lily May like a brick and she realized Mr. Erne hadn't stopped for breakfast on the way to the school. She was *starving*.

"Elle, this is Lily, East Wing." Mrs. Duran called to the dark-haired woman currently bent over an oven pulling out a rimmed tray of food.

Again, the mingled aromas of hot food washed over Lily May.

Elle put the tray on the center island, placing it carefully onto two ceramic tiles meant to disperse heat, and turned to looked at them. She flicked her head to toss her ponytail to the back and wiped a sleeve across her brow.

"Well this one's just a tiny bird, isn't she?" She wiped her hands on her apron, as she approached.

Lily glanced at Tommy spoke to him in her inner voice. *She ain't but a pound over skinny, but thinks I'm thin?*

He shrugged, as he wandered around the kitchen looking into the pans set out on counters.

Lily knew Tommy couldn't smell the aromas and wondered if he could remember the smells just by seeing certain things. Did a ghost remember what their favorite food tasted like? Or just that it was their favorite?

"I leave her to you." Mrs. Duran turned and went out the door they had entered, paying no heed to the IN and OUT signs.

"Lily, eh? Pretty name. I'm Elle Goodman. Somewhere in the pantry is Ava Sanders, can't miss her. She looks like she ate the last cook."

"I heard that!" A voice came from the back corner where Lily May saw the open door of a pantry.

"We're not Missus or Miz in here, we're just Elle and Ava, okay? I'm the cook. She's laundry, but she helps out at breakfast and lunchtime. The rest of the help I get comes from y'all." She nodded to a list on the wall behind the door. "We do a round robin of sorts with the students here. We'll just put you into rotation Sunday when we start the next week. Then you'll be on kitchen duty, help Ava with the laundry, and even clean bathrooms on occasion."

"Really?" Lily May hadn't expected to have chores like she did at home.

"Absolutely, little bird. We're going to teach you more than math here, dearie."

— f·o·u·r —

After a quick tour of the kitchen, pantry, and the laundry facilities in the basement, Lily May was shooed out to the cafeteria to eat with the rest of her classmates. She was still reeling from the fact the school was big enough for an elevator—an elevator which went from the laundry room, up through the kitchen, and up further into an access running along the library. Neither Caroline nor the dean had shown her the access hallways, but it was a big school and she was sure there was plenty more she hadn't seen yet.

Lily May devoured her plate of chicken casserole with rice and green beans, and was delighted to find she could go back for seconds.

Caroline was stunned she had anywhere to put that much food. "But you're so skinny." Caroline's eyes widened as Lily May finished off a full second helping.

Lily considered Caroline unspoken question. *Real food. I haven't had real food in weeks. Just watery canned soup the man fed me when he remembered.*

But Caroline didn't know about the man and the basement. She didn't know anything at all about what Lily May had been through, what she had survived, and Lily May didn't feel like explaining it at the moment. She shrugged and dragged the last bit of her bread through the gravy on the plate before popping it in her mouth.

"I ain't been eating well lately. I'm just real hungry."

"It's okay, I was just teasing you. I'm sorry. You must have enough to worry about being away from family and home and all the crazy of this place." Caroline put a hand on Lily's shoulder and smiled at her as sweet as a child who wanted cookies before dinner.

After they were finished, Caroline taught her how to bus her own dishes before leading her out with the rest of the students.

"We have just enough time for a bathroom break before grabbing our math books from upstairs. Do you need to pee?" Caroline walked toward the stairs, passing the bathroom to the left of the dining hall.

"I... yes?" Lily May looked back at the bathroom behind her.

"We'll use the ones upstairs. They're bigger, and nicer."

"Oh my goodness. Who's *that*?" Lily May stopped and turned toward a boy sitting on the chair by the nurse station desk. His hand, held up to cover his eye and most of his cheek, obscured the student's face. Lily May could see blood between his fingers and wondered if it came from his eye or a flesh wound near it. She was as horrified by his appearance as she was with the fact she couldn't hear *his* thoughts either, even though he was obviously in distress.

Caroline looked over and shrugged. "I don't know. Must be a West Winger." She continued toward the stairs but stopped at the bottom. Two steps up was a young woman with long brown hair, her straight-cut bangs barely touching the edge of her silver glasses. "Hey, Ms. Pond."

Caroline turned back to Lily May, "This is one of our teachers."

"Lillian Holloway?" The teacher was soft spoken, almost fragile sounding.

"Lily May, please, ma'am."

Ms. Pond nodded, "Come with me."

"Oh wow. I forgot how much first day sucks, but it's almost done." Caroline patted Lily May's shoulder before moving past Ms. Pond and continuing up the stairs. "See ya later. *Again*."

After a brief stop at the bathroom, Lily May found herself in what Ms. Pond referred to as the Assembly Room, across the hall from the nurse's station. Several rows of chairs faced the front of the room where two long tables were placed near the wall, with chairs behind them and a podium between them. Ms. Pond put Lily May at the table nearest the door they'd entered and opened the binder she'd been carrying. She set a pack of stapled papers down next to Lily May, moving the first of the stack over and placing it in front of Lily May, she lay a pencil on top of it.

"We're going to have you take a couple placement tests, so we know for sure what classes to put you in. Especially because we're near the end of the year and we need to know if we're moving you forward or keeping you back. We wouldn't want to stunt your education while we're sharpening your other talents."

Mr. Pond moved to the second table and set the binder down. She settled into the middle chair, opening a novel Lily hadn't noticed she was carrying. "And don't worry, none of these are timed. Take as long as you need, *within reason*. If you're stumped, just move on past it. It's not a grade so much as a *guide* for us."

"Yes ma'am." Lily May looked at the page in front of her and sighed. *Algebra*.

The next several hours were filled with quizzes and questions across a variety of subjects. She thought she did okay on the English and math portions, but worried because she'd never been good at history and felt she'd failed that section completely.

The blur of papers and time eventually led to a *fantastic* dinner of beef roast and red potatoes. Lily regarded the salad station with disdain, ignoring it except to pull a scoop of raw cauliflower onto her plate. After dinner she noticed a couple students headed into the kitchen and presumed they must be on the roster for kitchen help. The rest of the crowd filed out of the cafeteria and up the stairs with chatter and banter between them. Some went to their rooms. Caroline ushered Lily May to the lounge, several others entering before and after them.

"Do you shower in the morning or at night?"

"I usually take my bath before bed." Lily May glanced around the large room.

The far end of what was essentially a group living room had a flat screen television surrounded by two extra long couches and several bean bag chairs. The area near the door had three round table and chair sets like the dinette Tommy's mamma and papa had, though these were a smooth polished wood rather than the stained and cracked laminate back in Tommy's kitchen. Along the wall behind the tables were bookshelves stacked with board games and puzzles. Caroline walked to the second table, swiping a pack of cards from the shelf as she passed it. She sat down and squinted at Lily May.

"Baths? Really?"

"Yeah. I like to sink down with my head under water where the world is quiet 'cept for my own heartbeat."

"The only bath we have here is the sick tub in the nurse's station."

Lily May knew exactly the size and use of such a tub, and recalled the vague memories she had of being shoved into an ice bath when she had scarlet fever in preschool. She shuddered involuntarily. "A shower is fine. But nighttime is better, if I get to choose."

"Cool, I'm a morning girl."

"Hey Caroline." The light-haired boy from earlier sat down. His dark spikey-haired friend followed, pulling out the remaining of the four chairs. "And the new girl."

"Lily." Lily May offered and smiled. "And you're... Sam?"

"No, I'm Sam." The dark-haired boy smiled wide enough for Lily May to see most of his teeth. "He's Alex."

"Sorry." Lily May pulled in her lower lip.

"No worries. I bet you were told about a hundred names today." Alex turned to Caroline, "Did you rattle off everyone's names for her?"

Caroline answered with a silent look and long blink.

Lily wondered if it was just a deep friendship

between them or flirting. She found it was hard to tell when she couldn't hear the longing. Alex had some, but Caroline's thoughts were blocked from Lily, so she didn't know if it was reciprocated, or if Caroline even knew. But she could tell the mood was light and she relaxed, laughing softly, "Maybe not a hundred."

"Hey, I asked for name tags my first week." Sam slapped Alex's arm. "Remember that?"

Alex nodded without smiling and turned to Lily May, "Don't worry. You'll remember soon enough. And then you'll probably want to forget a few."

"That is a *wicked* bruise on your face. Does it hurt?" Sam leaned closer and inspected Lily's jaw.

Lily May swallowed and shook her head to answer, though the movement was barely more than a tremor. She couldn't tell if the boy was impressed with her fortitude or upset by the mark of violence.

"It's a good healing color, even has some yellow at the edges already. It'll be cleared up in a couple days." Alex looked her up and down, "And those ribs will be better by the end of the month." He winked at her and snatched the cards from Caroline's hand, as if knowing she didn't want to talk about any of it and purposely stopping his friend from further prodding. "Rummy?"

"Do you know how to play Rummy?" Caroline asked, and Lily May shook her head no. "Wanna learn?"

"Can I just watch for a bit?" She shrugged and paused her gaze on each of them in turn, wondering what abilities, powers, skills or talents they might each have. She wanted to ask, but felt it was pushy for the first day. She'd likely learn soon enough.

Without any homework holding them back, the three of them played Gin Rummy, finally convincing her to try. It felt good to be surrounded by kids who didn't shun her or shame her. For the first time in her life, Lily May's environment felt warm and inviting around people other than her mamma and meemaw.

Kals and Odette joined and watched, but didn't play.

Tommy settled onto the unoccupied end of the couch and watched television. Occasionally yelling out to Lily May about what was happening on the show.

Caroline eagerly introduced Lily May to Miko. The girl had long black wavy hair, red glasses, and what Lily May's meemaw would call *Indian cheekbones*. She smiled and was polite to Lily May, but seemed upset as her eyes darted around the room. Miko scampered off to bed not long before a tall Hispanic boy came to the lounge doorway and announced it was curfew.

He scanned the room, and Lily May noticed he stopped on each of them for a beat, like a bus driver taking a silent headcount. "Shower if you're going to, otherwise, off to your rooms."

"Oh yeah, we have to get you towels and toiletries. Come on, I'll show you. They're in the linen closet in the access hall." Caroline motioned for Lily May to follow her, and turned to Carlos for approval. He nodded and smiled at Lily May with a knowing look that made her think either Carlos had seen her file, or he somehow *knew* what she'd gone through.

A shrill alarm woke Lily May abruptly and she jumped from her bed in a panic, expecting to at least *smell* the smoke if not see the flames. She blinked several times as her eyes adjusted. Tommy was standing by the door frantically waving for Lily May to join him and leave the room. Caroline was still sleeping soundly.

Lily May rushed to her roommate's bed and shook the girl. "Caroline! There's a fire! Wake up!"

Caroline rolled toward her and squinted one eye open as if a bright light were shining into her face. "Wha—?" Her eyes went wide and Lily May knew the girl had registered the alarm screaming for her attention.

Caroline hopped out of her bed and grabbed the backpack hanging from the corner post. "Let's go!" She headed straight for the door with Lily May on her heels.

Lily May had never heard an alarm so loud and wondered if it was because it was shrieking in the otherwise silence of the night, or if the large corridors created some sort of echo chamber, like the natural caverns she'd visited once on a school field trip. She ran into the back of Caroline as the girl stopped at the door rather than opening it.

"Sorry." Lily mumbled, eyes wide.

"Shhh…" Caroline snapped at her and put her hand against the door, closing her eyes, she appeared to be concentrating. "There's no heat and I can hear others in the hallway. Come on." She spoke to Tommy rather than Lily May as she pulled the door open and stepped out.

The bright overhead lights, which kept the enormous building lit throughout the day, were apparently turned off at night. Lily May looked up in the dim hallway to find small sconce style lights between every other door. She likened them to nightlights, though they were above her head rather than at her ankles like the shell-shaped one in the bathroom at home. Unlike the brighter white of the main light fixtures, these were an amber color like the bug light Papa had put on the front porch. The effect left the whole area in heavy shadow, which was likely enough to get to the bathroom on any given night, but combined with the screaming siren, was far from comforting.

Lily May squinted into the darkness and saw no fire. There was nothing but startled students—some clutching pillows, others clinging to other possession they'd grabbed on the way out the door. Lily May thought of Meemaw's quilt and wished she'd have thought to take it.

The gathering of students acted as a wave, pushing the group as a whole, like a school of fish. Shuffling feet and whispered concerns made the hall seem loud, but Lily May realized she was catching all the *inner* voices in heightened states of anxiety.

Several teachers had come from their rooms. Lily May noticed a couple move toward the West Wing, as two others came straight at her group. She still could not smell smoke and wondered if they were going to be turned around to use the back stairs. After all, they had no idea which way was safe.

"Carlos?" Mr. Erne approached the group of children, pausing to pat both Caroline and Lily May's shoulders in a reassuring manner. "Carlos?" He searched over the heads of the children until he spotted the boy near the back.

"I'm here, Mr. Erne."

Lily May turned and watched the Hispanic boy make his way through the crowd.

Carlos had shooed them off to bed hours ago, but appeared as if he'd had a full night's sleep already. The boy next to Carlos, however, appeared to be more than tired—he seemed downright weary in his crumpled, dirty pajamas. It took Lily May a moment to recognize he wasn't a student, but rather the ghost she'd seen cross the hall earlier, and the dirt on his pajamas was soot. He looked her way, and she nodded as she made direct eye contact, letting him know she could indeed see him. Mr. Erne's voice, booming next to her to be heard over the alarm, startled her, and took her attention from the boy.

"Emergency headcount and lockdown." Mr. Erne and a female teacher Lily May hadn't met yet, both held up their hands to motion the students to stop their forward surge, and Mr. Erne continued giving directions. "Everyone go to your room, and stand outside until your room is cleared."

"Mr. Erne?" Carlos furrowed his brows.

"We've got a missing student in the West Wing."

"Ah, gotcha." Carlos nodded and gave Mr. Erne a thumbs up, as if that was all the information he needed. Lily May heard his unspoken commentary. *Another one?*

Lily May took his thoughts to mean it had happened before and the boy knew the exact protocol. His calm demeanor and immediate call to action helped Lily May understand why they not only *had* a lead dorm monkey, as Caroline had called him, but that Carlos was indeed fit for the job.

Carlos turned to the group of students, "All right, you heard the man. No fire. Everything is fine. Go back to your rooms and stand outside to wait for me. I'll be there as I get there." He turned back to Mr. Erne, and Lily May heard him ask softly, "Is it someone dangerous? Or in danger?"

Mr. Erne pursed his lips for a moment considering the situation, "Let's hope not."

"Come on." Caroline pulled on Lily May's arm and stepped back to their doorway.

The other children did the same, positioning themselves on either side of their doors. Lily May saw the mean girl from earlier, *Alyssa*, lean her head back against the wall and give off an exaggerated sigh, as if this was an inconvenience to her and she didn't care about anyone being missing or hurt. Further down, Lily May saw two boys slide down the wall and sit on the floor. One looked around at his classmates, the other pulled his knees up tight and laid his head down against them. Carlos walked through all of them to the other end and started with the room Sam and Alex shared. Lily May watched Carlos go into the room for a few moments then come back out and speak to the two boys. They went inside and shut their door. Carlos wrote something on their white board and moved to the next room.

"Might as well sit. It's going to be a while."

Caroline slid down to the floor and crossed her legs in front of her.

"What is all this?" Lily May joined Caroline on the floor but didn't look at her with the question, instead keeping her gaze down the dim hall on the other students. "What does missing mean? Did they run away? Are they dead? What's *missing*?" Lily May's mind raced at the possibilities, her imagination getting darker and darker to match her anxiety of being in the strange location with an alarm in the dead of night.

"Whenever someone goes *missing*—meaning they're not where they're supposed to be, or dawdling in the bathroom, or if maybe some of their stuff is also gone—they do a full building check and shutdown. They'll go through every single room and clear it, hopefully finding the student along the way. They usually find them in someone else's room, where they shouldn't be, and then we all get a talk about the birds and bees and rules of the dorms."

"Birds and b—" Lily May held back a snicker. "Ohhh…"

"Yup, young love, as my dad calls it. Happens every couple of years, usually right after graduation when all the kids cycle through and there's no one left to remember the trouble it caused last time."

Lily May smirked and watched the action down the corridor. The alarm stopped and as its echo faded, the air in the hallway seemed to suddenly have a pulse. The whispers between students weren't nearly as loud as their inner thoughts. She knew she wasn't supposed to listen, but Lily May paid attention.

A boy named Drake had pulled the name Jezzy from Mr. Erne's mind. He had whispered the information to his roommate, but several nearby students had also heard it, and within moments the name had been passed from door to door as the students spread speculation. She heard the fear in their thoughts and turned to Caroline.

"Jezzy?" Lily May whispered, seeing Kals sit up taller across the way and lean forward to pay attention. Odette, her roommate, had closed her eyes and her breathing made Lily May think she'd somehow actually fallen asleep in the chaos.

"Oh no..." Caroline's eyes widened and she looked down the hall, eyes flitting across the students. "That's not good at all. She's a pusher. A wicked pusher."

"Jezebel?" Kals pushed a hoarse whisper across the corridor.

"What do pushers do?" Lily May's eyes darted back and forth between the girls, hearing Kal's fearful thoughts jumble around themselves, but still unable to hear anything internal from Caroline.

Caroline looked around her, as if checking the area because she was about to share a secret. "Depends on the pusher. Some can affect electronics, some can heat themselves up and the things they touch, others can move objects—"

"And some are psycho." Kals interrupted. "We know all about her because the teachers don't trust her and don't think they can control her, and well, we have spies who can hear those thoughts. Jezzy is a suggestive, Lily May. She can tell you what to do and you just... *do* it."

Caroline's head bobbed up and down in agreement as she added, "Worse, she can stand right in front of you and tell you *not* to see her and you won't. My dad says they're working on a way to prevent that. To either stop abilities like that, or protect yourself by learning how to block them out."

"*Enough* gossiping, girls." Ms. Pond appeared from the foyer to enter the dorm corridor, a male teacher at her side.

The woman's long hair was in a ponytail, her bangs disheveled, and her glasses missing. Lily May, still getting used to all the new names and faces, almost didn't recognize her as the teacher who'd given her the pile of placement tests. Ms. Pond stopped by the girls and leaned against the wall of the lounge with her arms crossed. The man continued past them. Lily May watched him walk down the corridor and turn into the back stairwell. Glancing back to Ms. Pond, she realized the woman had positioned herself to be able to see both the length of the dormitory hallway, as well as the foyer stretching between and connecting the East and West Wing.

The presence of an adult effectively hushed the whispers in the dim lights, but Lily May could still hear several *inner* voices. *Not everyone's though,* she noted, and looked from face to face trying to discern which she could hear and which were silent, blocked from her like Caroline's. As Carlos cleared the room next to his and the two boys turned to go inside, the shorter one turned toward Lily May and made eye contact. She met his gaze and heard his thoughts clear as day.

Be careful.

Lily May made a mental note to ask Caroline who that was and what his abilities were. She didn't think she pulled the thoughts from him so much as he pointblank said it directly to her.

Carlos cleared one room at a time, Caroline and Lily May's being the last of them. As the two of them went inside, shutting the door as instructed, Lily May realized there was no lock.

"Should we set a chair in front of the door? To block it somehow?"

Caroline crawled into bed and squinted at Lily May. "It's a small school filled with people who can read minds. There's a reason locks were deemed *unnecessary*. There's no theft or misbehavior with the belongings of others, because there's almost zero chance of getting away with it." She yawned and lay back against the pillow. "And rules say we can't put anything in front of the door. Fire hazard or something." She turned away from Lily May. "Go back to sleep. They've got this."

Lily May sat on the edge of her bed and thought about the fear and anxiety she'd heard in the hallways when the missing child's name had been discovered. The dull panic of a possible fire rushing everyone to the stairs was suddenly escalated by the possibly of a pusher being in one of their rooms. As Caroline's breathing slowed to a peaceful slumber, Lily May's mind raced.

It's nice to not be alone anymore. Guilt for the thought flitted through Lily May's heart and she looked around for Tommy, finding him curled up and also sleeping—or doing what he called *ghost napping*—at the end of her bed. Her mind went back into overdrive.

I guess I knew deep down there must be others like me, 'specially after Tommy and me found each other. But a whole school of 'em? And then learnin' other abilities are real, too? Not just some crazy person pretending or a fancy movie? Kids, people, with abilities. But not just like me. Not like mine. There are people who can tell you what to do? Who can force you to do a thing? And others who can move stuff or start fires?

Lily May's mind ran out of control as she replayed every movie or book she'd ever seen or read about mental skills and psychic abilities. She scooted back on her bed and leaned against the wall, thinking about the repercussions of this revelation. She imagined Papa would have reacted awful to this reality. She wondered how on earth they could teach them all to use their powers and not instill fear in everyone they met.

In the silence, she considered the students around and realized she wasn't alone with abilities, but she was left alone by the dead looking to *use* hers. The absence of the dead struck her suddenly and she smiled.

There are only three dead here, other than Tommy, and not a one of 'em knows me or what I can do. Not a one of 'em interrupted me brushing my teeth or stood at the end of my bed askin' for me to go fetch a jar of pennies they hid and give it to their kin, or to pass on the location of a key or nothin'. Nothin'. Other than Tommy, I ain't got no dead buggin' me.

She sighed and appreciated the silence around her, even as her mind continued to work through everything she'd done and learned during the day. She sat up thinking well past the room check, and long after the hall had been free of any and all noise from the teachers. She assumed the girl had been located, and her feet were as restless as her mind, so Lily May opened the door to wander her new surroundings. New slippers still in the closet, she headed out barefoot.

She didn't get very far.

Outside the library, a suite door opened and startled Lily May. Turning with an audible gasp, she saw Ms. Pond—hair no longer in a pony and even *more* disheveled than earlier—coming out of one of the rooms in what Caroline had said were the male teacher's suites. The two froze and stared at each other for a moment.

Was the teacher up talkin' about the missing girl with someone? Lily May wondered about the nature of the visit, but Ms. Pond's inner voice told her how very wrong she was. *Oh... oh my.*

This was longing, and Lily May knew all about longing. It was one of the strongest emotions people couldn't keep to themselves. Anger, sadness, turmoil, and longing were the things Lily May had the most difficult time *not* hearing. They were so loud.

And Ms. Pond's longing was all but screaming at Lily May in the silent hallway.

Ms. Pond blushed as she broke the silence, quickly approaching Lily May. "What are you doing out here, Lillian?"

"Sorry ma'am, I couldn't sleep." Lily May didn't bother correcting the woman about her name, as long as it would take her to remember everyone, it would likely take them a bit as well.

Ms. Pond approached and put her hands on Lily's shoulders before gently turning Lily May toward the dorms, and nudging her gently. "Off to bed with you. I know the first day can be exciting and overwhelming, but you need to get some sleep."

Lily May turned and regarded the woman, wondering if Ms. Pond really thought that was the only thing on Lily May's mind. *There's a student missing,* she thought, but heard nothing about the girl in the teacher's thoughts. Only longing, and embarrassment. Lily May left her without a word and returned to her room, hearing a door open and close behind her, but not turning around to see if Ms. Pond had returned to her dalliance, or her own room.

— s · i · x —

Lily May had been given a schedule after her placement tests had been assessed. A quick comparison to Caroline's showed they were in all the same classes, and the girls squealed with delight.

Caroline gathered her things to grab her morning shower. "So the way it works in the morning is this. They start serving breakfast at seven and our first class is at eight. If you shower in the morning, like me, you can either eat before or after, and we've all kind of fallen into habits and patterns with each other. I eat after my shower, because they don't like us to wander in our PJs, and I feel like getting dressed just to get *redressed* is weird. " Caroline held a small purple bucket with a handle. Inside it, Lily May saw shampoo, soap, a loofa, toothbrush and toothpaste. Fresh clothes and a towel were tucked under her arm. "You can go down and eat now if you want, or you can wait for me. It's up to you."

"I best wait here."

"Cool, I'll be back." Caroline skipped from the room and Lily May smiled at the door as it closed. The girl seemed to *always* be happy.

Lily May turned and surveyed the room she finally had to herself. She had unpacked her meager belongings the night before—pants and underclothes into the dresser drawers, shirts and dresses hung in the closet, with the small brown suitcase next to her shoes on the floor. All said, she only had six outfits with her and the choice wasn't a difficult one. She grabbed the soft blue knee-length dress hanging in the closet.

She hadn't seen any other children in dresses, or even skirts, the day before, but then again, she was displaced in both location and fashion from what she'd grown up knowing. Mrs. Duran had mentioned a shopping trip in the coming days, where she would take Lily May to get her more clothes, a couple different options for shoes—stating she'd need something different for gym class—and other essentials. Lily May honestly couldn't remember the last time she'd even gone on a shopping trip. Even her yearly school clothing wardrobe had always been collected over the summer at local garage sales. *New* clothes—not hand-me-down or homemade—were foreign to Lily May, but she looked forward to it with excitement.

She dressed and flipped through the stack of books she'd been given the day before, as she waited for Caroline to return from her shower. Tommy, who'd politely turned away while she dressed, sat next to her on the bed and looked over her shoulder while she perused her schedule.

There were six *study blocks* listed, with some topics being taught together. English and math seemed to be alone and concentrated. Social studies included psychology, history involved philosophy, science came with both forensics and law, and physical education included the athletics of gym class with the bookwork of health, and also alternated days with music. It sounded like a full day of school crammed into forty-five minute increments and all done by three in the afternoon. Lily May wasn't sure when exactly they were going to teach her about her abilities, and wondered if it was something between classes and dinner.

Caroline arrived already dressed and tucked her shower caddy into the corner of her closet. She turned to find Lily sitting on the bed with her hands under her thighs while her legs bounced lightly against the mattress.

"You hungry?" Caroline raised an eyebrow at her.

"Absolutely." Lily patted her stomach and hopped from the bed.

Three steps into the hall, Caroline turned and looked down at Lily's bare feet. "Um, did you forget your shoes?"

Feeling like a fool, Lily scurried back to the room and grabbed her scuffed navy blue slip-on flats. She'd hoped either Caroline wouldn't notice, or would tell her barefoot was fine. She got neither and sighed.

A quick breakfast—Caroline having taken longer to get showered and dressed than Lily May had anticipated—allowed for only a smattering of questions, as the majority of the meal was laden with whispers and rumors regarding the missing girl from the night before.

"She must have been found," Caroline had assured her among the speculations. "Otherwise they usually call us to Assembly."

"But they won't tell us what happened?" Lily May's gaze slid across the room. Only a handful of students were present and she imagined the rest had all eaten and were back in their rooms waiting for class.

"Nah. She's West Wing. Doesn't matter to us what they're doing." Caroline spoke with a mouth full of bacon. "They keep us apart and they don't share much between the wings at all."

"And that's okay?"

"Sure, why not?" Caroline shrugged. "Now come on, we're gonna be late for English class."

Rushing upstairs, again choosing the second

floor bathroom for a quick stop, Caroline and Lily May gathered their books.

"You can kick those off now if you want." Caroline nodded at Lily's feet.

"Truly?"

"Absolutely. There's actually no *rules* about shoes except in the cafeteria because of health reasons, oh and while we're outside you probably should wear them. As long as we're all showering and keeping clean, no one is running outside through the mud or neighboring pastures, there's nothing wrong with it. Like my dad says, it's your *house*, be comfortable." Caroline winked and waited for Lily to slip from her shoes before they hurried back down toward the classrooms.

Going into the first classroom on the right, Lily May's internal compass was beginning to acclimate and she realized they were directly below their room and the student lounge. Students were already in their seats, two per table, in a room with several rows of tables rather than individual desks.

"You can sit with me." Caroline sat at a table in the second row and pointed to the empty seat. Lily May had barely settled into the chair, scooting it closer to the table, when the teacher entered the room.

Ms. Pond made eye contact with Lily May and immediately turned her gaze away. Lily

May tried her damnedest to not hear things, but Ms. Pond's embarrassment was a type of turmoil, and *almost* as loud as the longing had been. Lily caught how the teacher wasn't ashamed of the relationship she was having with whomever had been in that room. She was far more concerned that Lily May had heard her specific thoughts about him. Lily had no way to reassure her otherwise until class was over, but smiled when she got the chance and tried to act clueless to alleviate the teacher's fears.

The class hour was about 19th Century American Poets and Lily was pleased to be familiar with the poem of the day, *Oh Captain, My Captain*. The class went rather quickly, while Lily May took furious notes, knowing she'd have reading to catch up later.

English was followed by social studies with Mr. Pence, a sharp looking man in his mid-thirties with a short military-style haircut and pressed dress shirt poking out of a sensible but lightweight sweater. Lily May quickly learned several things. This class would include not only psychology as taught in books, but in regards to how people react to those with abilities. Lily May also learned he was brokenhearted and had recently left someone who hurt him to the core—he had both longing *and* pain.

History was with Keith Williamson, a soft-spoken black man who was a previous student.

He came back to teach so he could help the next generation, and included philosophy with his history lessons. As far as Lily May could tell, he scratched his mustache when waiting for a student to answer a question, and the philosophy portion was mostly inline with the textbooks, rather than how it pertained to abilities.

The last class before lunch was science, and it quickly became Lily's favorite. Not only was she pleased to see Mr. Erne as the teacher, but the class itself was full of powerful information and direction for those with talents. Mr. Erne smiled with approval when Lily May automatically sat down next to Caroline.

"Welcome to class, Lily May. I hope your second day is a bit more of what you expected than the first." His eyes moved under the table and he saw she was barefoot. A tiny smile escaped the left side of his face.

She smiled wide at him, delighted and relieved to know he would be one of her teachers. He gave Caroline a slight nod and turned to the rest of the class.

"Because we have a new student, we're going to throw the planned curriculum out the window and take the hour to discuss the finer points of what we do in this school."

A wave of murmurs went through the other students who seemed to be in all of Lily May's classes with her. Four boys and four girls all gave muted cheers to Mr. Erne's announcement.

"And how many of you have had the chance to introduce yourself or meet Miss Lily May?" Mr. Erne scanned the room.

Several hands shot up and Lily May checked them. She did indeed know Caroline, Kals, Odette, Miko, Sam and Alex, if only on the surface. But she hadn't run into the other two boys, who not only left their hands down, but shook their heads to confirm their answer.

"Well, let's start with introductions. And you know how I feel, this isn't names only, tell the girl what you can do and make her feel welcome. Lily May has lived most of her life not being accepted, let's change that." He sat and pushed his leather planner to the side of his desk. "I'll start."

Lily May's mouth opened in shock. *Mr. Erne has... powers? How didn't I know that?*

"As the rest of you know, I can see blood from the past. As a child, I referred to it as *ghost blood*, because it stayed behind no matter how much cleaning was done. It made hospitals very difficult for me, and truth be told, I struggled to find a career that wouldn't make me crazy. Turned out, if I used the ability on the job, things worked out better. For a time, I worked with local police in forensics and on an advisory level with homicide."

"You see blood that's not there?" Lily May's

expression twisted into confusion.

"Yes. For instance, you once cut your fingertip and the blood ran down your finger and into your hand."

Lily May looked at the open palm of her hand, remembering the time the drinking glass broke on her while doing dishes. The suds and water thinned her blood and it ran freely down to puddle in her hand. "But that was years back."

"Yes, and you cleaned it up well that day, I'm sure. You've also washed your hands hundreds of times since then. But I can still see it when I look at your hand."

"Oh Lord…" Lily May was still staring at her hand imagining the horror of seeing *ghost blood* everywhere. "But how do you—"

"I can tell the difference now. I couldn't always. I had to learn that. I can also tell approximately how old it is by the color. You hurt yourself about five years ago, right?"

Lily May nodded in awe.

"See? You're not alone. Other people have things they can do that they have to live with. In here, and several of your other classes, we'll teach you how to use it, control it if need be, and make it useful. Let's move to Caroline now." His eyes flicked toward Lily May's roommate with a loving smirk.

She whispered, "I see dead people." The class giggled but Lily May didn't know why. "Oh, sorry. It's from a movie I'm guessing you haven't seen. It's up in the lounge's movie collection, we can watch it later if you want."

"Caroline…" Mr. Erne urged her to focus.

"Oh yeah, so, I see ghosts, like Tommy. And if I'm in the area where they died, I can actually see their demise play out. Remember the little boy who crossed the hallway in front of us yesterday?"

Lily May nodded, remembering Caroline's delight at Lily May being able to see him.

"When he gets through the other side, he falls and chokes to death from the smoke. That happens in what is Shane and Keagan's room. I saw it one summer when everyone was gone for break and it made me so sad I cried for days, so I just don't go in there."

Mr. Erne tilted his head slightly at Caroline and narrowed his eyes.

"I don't go in *any* boy's room." She gave Mr. Erne a sideways glance.

At the next table, Kals spoke to move things along, "Kaleigh, but Kals by most." She flashed a wide grin that was the purest smile Lily had ever seen, even if it was full of crooked teeth. "I'm what they call a hyper empath. I can sense the emotional and mental state of other people, but I also get little flashes of traumatic events if they've had any. It's kind of like I see quick snapshots, still pictures, in my head, *not* video."

"Odette, and I'm psychometric. I can touch people and see major events. So sometimes, depending on whether it was traumatic or not, Kals and I can get the same info from someone. Other times I'll see it because it's important to them, but she won't because it's not necessarily traumatic. Also, I can feel their emotions and have to pull back from that and follow their social cues so I don't overstep into someone's private feelings. Of course, I'm only level *one*. I touch the person and know things. Alyssa—the senior—she's the other way. She can touch items and know the location of the owner. She's kinda mean sometimes, but someday she'll hopefully help find missing kids."

"Miko," the quiet voice came from the table behind Odette and Kals. The dark-haired girl with the red glasses and skittish behavior rose her hand to motion she was talking. "I can hear ghosts... but I cannot see them. Which is really scary and horrible."

Caroline leaned closer to Lily May, "That's why she's afraid of everything. Tommy will freak her out, so keep that in mind." She looked past Lily and winked. Lily turned to see Tommy sitting by the window, listening to everyone with a big grin. He gave Caroline two thumbs up.

Lily May thought back to the night before in the lounge when Tommy was yelling to Lily May about what was on the television and Miko had been upset and pacing before she finally left. She had probably *heard* Tommy, but without seeing him, it likely sounded like voices yelling near her. "Oh, should I *tell* her about Tommy?"

"Later." Caroline turned behind her to Sam. "You're up."

"Sam. I'm a remote viewer. If I concentrate I can see something far away. Sometimes in another room or building, but I've also gone as far as my house back home and watched my parents eat dinner."

Lily May's brows furrowed. "That's kind of creepy."

"That's the general consensus. And if that freaks you out, my sister can do astral projection and just leave her body all together when she goes off snooping in other locations." He smiled wide and raised his eyebrows up and down several times.

"Alex," the light-haired boy who always seemed to be smiling at Caroline, drew Lily May's attention away from Sam. "I can do what they call Health View, but I call it Sick Sense, you know, like *sixth* sense, but sick instead." He grinned at his own joke. "I can tell when people are sick, or if there is something wrong. Like last fall when Sam was really sick. When I looked at him, there was like a weird glow around his throat. I told them that and after some tests, they ended up taking out his tonsils."

"Wow, that's really useful…" Lily May was impressed and whispered her reaction without meaning to.

"Yep, which is why I wanna work with little kids, like in the pediatric ward where they're too little and can't explain what's wrong, but maybe I can see it."

"I'm Shane," the red-haired boy she hadn't met yet spoke up. "I have a photographic scenic memory. Like Ms. Pond can remember what she read and on what page and where on the page, but I can walk into a room once and remember where every little thing was. I want to be a spy, but Mr. Erne says that's not the only use of my talents." His voice changed as he mentioned the teacher and Lily realized he was mimicking Mr. Erne's commentary.

Lily May heard Mr. Erne snicker in response, but kept her attention on the table at the back of the room.

"And I'm Keagan, the one with the haunted room." Lily felt bad for the boy with blonde hair and sad eyes. "Which kinda sucks because I have second sight, I can see the past so I can see what Caroline saw. I can also see the burned floorboards and walls, but I'm learning how to turn it off and on and can ignore it most days. I'm going to work with cops like Mr. Erne did."

"And that is your class, Lily May. We discuss our abilities and practice them with each other as often as you want, but do try and remember to allow people their privacy. With that in mind, Lily May, how about you tell us what you can do?"

Lily May stood and turned to the rest of the class, seeing their eager anticipation to find out what she could do. She felt simultaneously similar and vastly different from them.

None of 'em have accents or talk poorly like I sometimes do. They all sound like city kids from the television.

Lily *May* suddenly seemed so country and hick in this group of progressive kids.

"You can call me Lily. *Just* Lily. And I can hear the thoughts of the living, especially strong thoughts like love or pain." She glanced back at Mr. Erne, thinking of the stale sadness she'd heard from him in the car. He nodded and she realized he meant for her to continue. She turned back around and swallowed. "And I can talk to the dead."

"Woah, double powers…" Sam's eyebrows went up in genuine shock.

Mr. Erne talked over Sam's comment, ignoring the boy and dampening the effect of his words on Lily. "And there are other abilities out there, Lily. Our senior class includes a *touch emote* who can calm you with nothing more than a touch, as if absorbing your anguish, a *precog* who sees the near future, and a *telepath* not unlike yourself—that's what we call hearing thoughts." He looked over the students, "Now then, let's talk about how to use these abilities in your life, in a career, to feel fulfilled and help those around you."

The classroom began to talk at once, but Mr. Erne squashed their excitement and turned it into a calm discussion hour. Several of them had career paths figured out, others were still deciding. The options listed were everything from working with children to caring for comatose or catatonic patients, from detective work to social work. By the time the bell rang to let them know it was lunch, Lily not only knew her classmates better, she genuinely liked them.

Throughout the class, she caught glimpses of a man outside the window working on the bushes near the building. A gardener, Lily supposed. He glanced in the window occasionally and smiled. And when she accidentally caught his direct gaze, he simply nodded to her and continued trimming the tall evergreen column.

After lunch Caroline and Lily settled into Math class.

Just math, Lily thought. *And Algebra at that.*

Lily found herself bored after the excitement of Mr. Erne's class. This teacher, Ms. Jenna Hunt, had no abilities according to Caroline, and therefore didn't discuss them or even address them. She was *all* business.

The business of mixing numbers and letters in equations that don't make no sense most of the time. That's like putting peanut butter on hot dogs, it just don't belong.

But there was something else about the teacher, something deeper than her need for professionalism. At first Lily thought the teacher was bitter because she didn't have powers and was surrounded by extraordinary students. *Jealous?* But while Keagan was at the board doing a problem she'd written out, Ms. Hunt's mind wandered away from math and Lily heard the sadness and pain. This was loss, like heartbreak, but deeper, different.

When the bell announced the next class, Lily was still trying to work out what was going on with the teacher and wondering if it was tied to Mr. Pence's love loss. She decided it wasn't her business and she should try harder to stay out of the minds of her teachers and classmates.

Caroline hurried Lily up to their room to *dump the books* and wait for Lily to put her shoes back on, before they headed back down and through the hallway past all the classrooms. She burst through the door opposite the science room and into the sunshine.

"PE is back here." Caroline walked and talked excitedly without looking at Lily, instead she pointed at the building behind the main hall.

Lily noted a myriad of crisscrossing walking paths. The one they traveled on was very dark and looked freshly paved. It was wide enough to allow three or four students to walk side-by-side, and led to a set of double doors on the south side of the PE building Caroline had pointed to. Another paved path came from the West Wing and joined with theirs right before the double doors, making a large patch of pavement where they met. Their eastern path also crossed a single-lane road, which started at the exterior double doors of the kitchen and then wrapped around the building toward the front. Lily thought she'd seen where it came from by the roundabout. On the other side of the road, where the walkway started up again and resumed it's path to the PE building, an unpaved, worn-grass trail sprouted off about halfway and led to a smaller door on the right side of the building.

"You know..." Caroline glanced around at the surrounding students and whispered to Lily. "There's a tunnel under the West Wing that connects to the PE building. They used it during winter to avoid the weather, but it's been closed *forever*. I've never been in it or even seen it. Now if it gets too cold in the winter, they put up a weird plastic hood along the path—feels like you're going to some bizarre arctic research lab."

Around them, the grounds were green, lush, and neatly trimmed for several hundred yards in all directions. It was as if the building sat in the middle of an unused, but well cared for, golf course. Lily wondered why they'd cut the trees back so far. There was no outdoor equipment, but there was plenty of room for a track or tennis court or something of the sort in the massive expanse of lawn.

"PE, or gym class as some of the kids call it, is on Mondays, Wednesdays and Fridays. On Tuesdays and Thursdays we have music class out here. *Coach,* Mr. Fisher, used to be a music teacher—with no abilities other than perfect pitch—and really wishes those classes and days were flipped. But according to my dad, the *higher ups think exercise is more important than the violin*. I like Coach though, he's… well, he's casual. You'll see."

As Caroline and Lily approached, Lily saw double metal doors pulled open and held outward by other students. She noted the push-to-release bar handles like her old school had, and decided this building was much newer than the main hall, and very likely not part of the original boys' school. Inside, there were bathrooms to the left, followed by stairs leading down, and past that were two doors, the first hanging open. On the right was a closed set of double doors.

Caroline pointed at the double doors. "That's the gym." She walked further into the hall past the bathrooms, pointing again with little more than a dismissed wave, as they passed the stairs. "Those go down to the tunnel, we're not allowed down there. Music is up here."

She reached the first door and turned in. Lily followed and found it was actually two rooms with a divider between them. She'd seen the type of wall before, in the special meeting room at the Best Western. She'd gone there with her mamma to listen to some man in a light-colored suit talk about sharing the cost of a condo with other people in some other state. Lily asked what a condo was, and Mamma shook her head and told Lily they were only there for the free lunch and full day use of the hotel pool.

Inside the music room, folding chairs were arranged in several rows with a podium at the front of them. They weren't tightly organized like Lily had seen at the funeral parlor, but rather allowed plenty of room between each chair and each row. Lily hadn't taken orchestra or band in school, but she recognized the set up and knew the spacing was designed to allow for a music stand and whatever instrument you had.

She'd never played *any* instrument and had no idea where to sit. She froze at the doorway, sidestepping only when she realized there were students behind her trying to get in.

The children all filed in to their seats, settling in but not down. The group quieted as a squeak behind her caught Lily's attention. She spun and saw a young man with long brown hair pulled back in a low folded pony. He was pushing a cart with a television on the top and a squeaky wheel on the bottom. He stopped and used his foot to kick the door shut behind him.

He nodded to Lily and continued pushing the cart. "You must be Lily. Go ahead and sit anywhere today, we'll figure out your seat when we figure out your instrument." He plugged the machine in and turned back to the class, remote in hand. "We're not doing music today, we're watching a mandatory video on hygiene and hormones."

The classroom groaned as one.

"I know, Health is supposed to be on Gym days, but this is the makeup video from when the machine was broken. Let's just get it out of the way."

Mr. Fisher turned the overhead lights off in all but the back row, and pushed a button on the remote to start the video.

Lily immediately sat next to Caroline and leaned in close to whisper. "Tell me more about the tunnels."

"Tunnel. Just one." Caroline grinned, a twinkle of mischief in her eye. "It supposedly goes from those stairs in the hall to the basement below the West Wing. You know those back stairs we aren't supposed to use?"

Lily nodded.

"They go all the way to the basement, and both sides have one. So supposedly, at the bottom of those stairs is the tunnel. I thought someone got hurt and that's why they shut it down, but my dad said that wasn't why."

"Your dad knows a lot about this school—"

"I don't like these videos any more than you do." Mr. Fisher's voice interrupted and Lily slowly raised her eyes up to find the man standing right behind her and Caroline. "Let's not be *that* kind of new kid. Please pay attention. You are expected to pass the quiz afterward."

Lily felt her face flush with color.

"Sorry, Coach." Caroline flashed a smile far more innocent than Lily thought it actually was. The two girls snickered, and then watched the video in silence.

After class, walking back to their building, Lily had a clear view of the rear of McMillan Hall and the surrounding buildings. To the side where she'd seen the parking lot was a small cottage. She pointed and questioned Caroline.

"That's the headmaster's cottage. It's a nice little two bedroom where Mr. Landry can hide. Oh, he's got a tunnel, too! I forgot about that. I was only thinking of the ones the students used to have access to, but there is more than one. He's got one that goes to the basement as well, and likely for the same reason—winter. I wonder if his is shut down, too..." Caroline's voice trailed off and Lily noted her gait slowed while she was debating the idea.

"And what's over there?" Lily pointed to the small single story building on the other side of their East Wing. "I can see that one from our room."

Caroline blinked and followed Lily's finger beyond the main building, where the road from the kitchen wrapped around toward the front to disappear. "Super's shed. Well, shed and apartment, I guess."

"Super?"

"The superintendent, Patrick Malone. He's in charge of the non-teaching staff."

"Oh yes, Miz Yost told me about him." Lily nodded. "Or at least that he wasn't in charge of *her*."

Caroline laughed. "Sounds like Miz Yost. Mr. Malone was the maintenance man. Still is, actually. But when the last Super left, he had seniority so he got the job and the apartment that comes with it. So most of that building is maintenance stuff. There's a big door on the other side so they can drive the plow or lawn mower right out of it. And then this end of it is a little apartment."

Caroline paused for a moment and glanced back toward the headmaster's house. "Other than Mr. Malone and Mr. Landry, all the staff sleep inside the main hall with us. The teachers are on our floor, as is the dean. She's in the big room closest to our lounge. And then the other non-teachers have rooms on the third floor."

"Third floor?"

"Yep. The stairs go there, oh and the elevator, too. It's not the full size of the school though, it's only the middle section and just big enough for suites and a lounge."

"You've been up there?"

Caroline looked around. "Of course. We all

have. And you will too." She smiled. "Sneaking up there and getting something from their lounge is a rite of passage around these parts."

Lily panicked for a moment about stealing, but remembered the man outside the classroom window earlier. "So who was the guy outside during science class?"

"Which one? There's a groundskeeper, he's a cool older guy, and then we have a gardener, but I think he's only part-time or something because we rarely see him."

"It was an older guy. He was watching me through the window."

"Yup, definitely Mr. Young, but he'll insist you call him Warren because he thinks he's one of us. He's always watching, and seems to know when people are sick or missing. He's almost a guardian angel of sorts."

Lily saw Tommy suddenly walking on the other side of Caroline and wondered where he'd been.

"The gardener though. Wait until you see him. He's *soooo* cute." Caroline sped up to catch the door as another student went through it and let it go.

— e · i · g · h · t —

Lily had spent the first half hour of her post-dinner study time wandering the stacks of the library, her hand trailing along the spines of countless books. Her old school library could have fit in half of her dorm room, housing only donated paperbacks or volumes deemed necessary for the students to have access to, such as classics and an almost full set of the 1977 edition of Encyclopedia Britannica—missing volume six, Earth through Everglades.

Lily knew she came from a small poor town on the edge of nothing. The town was barely a blip on the map, and even then you'd have to squint, but her school had tried to make up for it with the Internet. And because not everyone had computer access at home, Harrison K-12 had offered computers for school use, as did McMillan Hall. The difference being, Harrison had two out-of-date clunky Dell machines with the letters worn off the keyboard and a tear in the mouse cord, while McMillan's computer

lab—tucked into the back corner of the library—
had a dozen state-of-the-art systems. She'd only
used the computer at Harrison for one project
the previous fall and knew almost nothing
about them. *Books* she knew, and the collection
of books on the shelves around her made her
heart flutter.

Lily had once visited the public library in
West Hope, but even that wasn't as big as this.
Larger than the dining hall, McMillan's library
was a thing of beauty, both in design and in
content. Gorgeous woodwork throughout the
room made it smell like a church. Even the
tables here were beautifully grained hardwood,
unlike the wood laminate folding tables used in
the cafeteria. There were several rows of floor-
to-ceiling bookshelves and three of the four
walls were massive bookshelves themselves,
all stretching up to the twelve-foot ceilings.
It was all accessible using either the short,
wheeled ladder along the outside wall or the
squat stepstools found in every other aisle.
Unlike Harrison's library, this one actually had
at least several shelves for each main section of
the Dewey Decimal System. Some of the books
appeared new, especially in the fiction area,
while others may have somehow survived the
fire and been around for nearly a century.

The back of the room was split, with the
computer lab closed off on the right for both

sound and privacy, and an L-shaped desk and small room to the left. The nameplate on the desk surprised her—Ms. Pond—but she supposed it made sense for the English teacher to also be the Librarian. An old card catalog sat against the outside wall of the tiny office and Lily smiled.

At least I know how to use that.

"Are you okay?" Tommy finally asked her. "You got a dumb look on your face."

She saw him sitting at one of the tables and gave him half a glance of annoyance. He'd barely learned to read when he'd died, so he'd always depended on her for stories. Looking around the library, Lily realized he didn't think there was anything here he'd care about.

"There might not be much for you in here, but I'll see what I can do, okay?"

He shrugged. "You gotta study now, right?"

She nodded, guilt creeping in for wasting time wandering the stacks.

"I'm gonna go see what Caroline's doing." He got up and scurried from the room, leaving Lily alone in the expanse of books.

The next few hours were a flurry of math worksheets and history reviews, both piles assigned with the promise of quizzes upon completion. The history was easy enough and more a review of what she'd already learned than anything new. But she struggled a little with the math and made notes to ask for help on a couple things. The American poets unit for English class was a breeze, and Lily finished her assignment before stretching her arms out with an exaggerated yawn.

She turned to check the time on the grandfather clock near the librarian desk, and was overcome with the same strange fuzziness she'd seen the first morning she'd been there. A strange fog seemed to swirl around the tall wooden clock. There was a shadow to the right side of the roman numerals of the face, like the wood was darker than it should be, and Lily believed the clock had been in the fire. She blinked away the fog and was startled to see a girl standing there, a look of fear on her face.

"Hello?" Lily spoke softly, presuming it was one of the seniors she hadn't met yet. The girl responded with widened eyes and a slack jaw.

Oh. Ghost. Lily knew they usually reacted with shock when they realized Lily could see them. Lily waved at the girl to indicate Lily was aware and unafraid.

The girl's strawberry blond hair was trimmed short, in what Meemaw called a pixie shag, and it fluttered slightly as she shook her head in an almost unseen motion. She mouthed something Lily couldn't hear and sidestepped to the computer lab, slipping into the open door and disappearing from view.

"Sorry." Lily spoke under her breath, feeling bad for startling the poor thing.

The clock read 9:25 and she knew curfew was coming soon. Lily gathered her books and papers, and headed back to her room.

"Hey Caroline." Lily pushed her door open and saw Caroline and Tommy sitting cross-legged on the bed, deep in conversation.

"Hi, Lily!" Tommy's enthusiastic expression was much better than the bored one he'd had in the library. "Caroline knows all kinds of good stories to tell me. And she remembers them, so she doesn't even need to read them from the books."

"Truly?" Lily put her books on the desk and sat on her bed across from the other two.

"I spent a lot of time alone as a child growing up around here, so all the teachers would buy me books to keep me company. I have them tucked away in storage if he wants them, but I know so many of them by heart, it's nothing to retell them from memory, or close enough at least."

"You growed up here?"

"Uh... sure. Um, going to school here and all."

Lily narrowed her eyes, wishing on all the stars she'd ever seen she could hear Caroline's thoughts.

Caroline blanched for a moment and Lily

could see she was considering something.

"You have to…" Caroline's expression twisted around fear and uncertainty. "Will you promise not to tell no one else?"

"Tell what?"

"Promise…" Caroline's eyes pleaded as much as her voice. Caroline swiveled her gaze to Tommy, imploring him with her expression only. Tommy nodded, eyes wide at the notion of a secret.

"Surely. I'd never tell somethin' if you don't want me to…"

Caroline looked at Lily and blinked several times, studying her. Caroline's mouth moved around wordlessly, and Lily could see the fear mingled with hope in her brown eyes. When she finally spoke, Caroline's cryptic comment came out in a cracked voice. "My last name is Erne."

Lily nodded and waited for the secret.

Caroline continued to watch her.

It took a couple beats for Lily's mind to catch up to Caroline's words. "Wait, Erne like Mr. Erne?"

Caroline nodded, her eyes welling up as if she were about to cry.

"Oh my goodness, Caroline. Is he your papa?" Lily leaned forward, her own excitement blurring the anxiety hanging in the air.

Caroline simply nodded, slowly, barely, as if afraid to admit it.

"Oh that's *wonderful*. He's so nice. He must be a great papa." Lily's bright, welcoming demeanor brought a smile to Caroline. "I really like him. But why is that a secret?"

"Because I don't want to be treated differently. I'm using my mom's maiden name on paperwork, but two of the seniors know, Preston and Drake, because they're like you, they heard it. But they've been instructed to keep it quiet." Caroline's lip curled up in crunched thought. "I'm surprised you didn't."

"I can't hear none of your thoughts." Lily shrugged.

"Not at all?"

Lily shook her head.

"We should tell my dad that. They'll want to figure out why that is and see if they can use it or change it. It's good for what they call their *case studies*."

Lily nodded. She didn't know what that exactly meant or what it would entail, but she liked Caroline *and* her papa, and trusted they wouldn't put Lily in danger.

"Have you all lived here since you was little?" Lily changed the subject back to Mr. Erne being Caroline's father.

"Not always. After Mom died, Dad tried his best. Grams helped when she could and there was daycare, of course. Eventually, I went to school. Dad was working for the police station then, fighting the good fight as he calls it, with his natural science and forensics degree, and *ghost blood*. But when I was about seven, I started seeing things. It turned out to be ghosts. Dad wasn't freaked out by it at all because of his own thing, and so he tried to help me."

Caroline swallowed hard and dropped her gaze to the floor. "Then I saw Mom. A bunch of times. She was sad but smiled *all the time*. She never spoke to me, not like Tommy does, just watched me. But a lot of them are like that, I can see them, but not talk to them."

"I seen that before. Usually 'cos they's newly passed or still learning how to be dead."

"Well, Dad had a real bad case at work. I mean *bad*. Said there was blood everywhere. And he couldn't do it anymore. He'd spent a lot of his youth avoiding jobs that *might* have blood echoes, which is what someone else once called it—maybe Mom—but after that case it didn't matter. It became all about me and how to help me deal with this the best I could. He found this place and applied. They'd never had someone with a child, but both of us being gifted, they wanted to embrace us and give us a home. Headmaster Landry is almost like a Poppy to me at this point, though I'd never dream of calling him that."

Caroline paused and looked around the room.

"I actually lived in Dad's apartment with him—he has the large suite on the other side—until last fall. I was moved over to the dorms when the last bunch of seniors graduated, after I turned fifteen. Before that, I had private classes from all the teachers and ate at different times, and like I said earlier, was really lonely so I read a lot."

"Well, now you're over here with the rest of 'em." She hopped off the bed and gave Caroline an impromptu hug before sitting next to her on the other girl's bed. "And me. And I promise not to tell…" Her voice trailed for a moment. "Can I tell your dad I know?"

Caroline nodded, her eyes glassy with what Lily thought was relief or happiness.

"Caroline, 'cos you been here since you was little, do you know who the ghost in the library is? It's a girl, but she don't talk none. Seemed awful shocked that I could see her."

"In the library?" Caroline furrowed her brows. "I didn't think there were any ghosts in the library. I don't think there's any girl ghosts in the whole school."

Lily contemplated a moment. "Maybe it's that third one I heard in the hall."

"Third?" Caroline raised an eyebrow.

"Why yes. When Mrs. Duran was giving me the tour and testing my abilities she said there were *two* ghosts, two boys who had died in the fire. But I could hear *three* distinct voices."

"Weird, I've never seen a third." Caroline shrugged. "Oh but speaking of ghosts, Tommy was telling me he died twice and you could talk to each other without talking after the *first* time he died. That's super cool. I mean, not that he *died*, but that it made him be able to do that. But he said he was dead again for a long time before you could see him."

"It *was* a long time. Months. Almost a year, I guess. And it was lonely. Tommy's my best friend. My only friend. And he was gone."

"You got him back, though."

"I did." Lily smiled at the small boy in the torn red shirt.

"But what happened to you guys right before Dad came for you?"

Lily's eyes glazed over for a moment. She recalled the dirty cellar she'd been held in for several weeks by the man who had taken her with the intent to kill her. She never wanted to talk about it again, but Caroline had shared her secret and told Lily about her papa. It seemed only fair to share something back.

"I was kidnapped by the man what killed Tommy, 'cos he thought I knew. But I didn't know until he tied me up and left me for days on end. I didn't know. Not 'til he told me I was gonna die, so's I might as well just tell him what I knew. But I didn't know…" Lily felt her throat tighten, remembering the fear she had in that cellar. In the dark. Alone. Until Tommy showed up.

"Tommy finally found me. Then he ran 'round town tryin' to get people to hear him or see him, to try and get me some help. But no one other than me could even see him. No one could hear him." She swallowed over a lump in her throat. "Before I was taken, my papa died. He was always afraid of me. He never liked me talking 'bout what I could do, and got *real* angry any time he thought I was listening to *his* thoughts. He blurred 'em with beer most of the time. After he died, I never saw his ghost. But Tommy spread the word through the dead I *did* know and someone found him. Told him. And he came for me."

"But he was a ghost…" Caroline's brows knit in confusion.

"He was. But Papa was just as strong and mean as he'd been when he was alive." Lily looked down, recalling the moments that led to her freedom. "He hopped inside me. Possessed me, I guess. Not for long, but long enough to hurt the man until he was unconscious, and then set me free. I ran and ran and ran. The cops caught the man, still bleeding and unconscious on his living room floor. And I never saw Papa again." She looked up to Caroline as a single tear rolled down her cheek. She sniffled. "I was still at the police station telling them what happened when your papa came to get me."

"Wait, they can possess people? Just jump into them and control them like puppets?" Caroline's eye went wide with excitement. "Oh my god, can Tommy do that? Can you hop inside me, Tommy? How would that feel?"

"No!" Lily shouted without meaning to and Caroline's expression changed to shock. "It's far too dangerous. It almost killed Papa. Tommy says last time he saw him he was fading and all blurry. We don't know if he got better or not. And Papa was *strong*. He was grown. Tommy is just little and not very strong at all. No way could he fight something as tough as a person's will. I lost him twice already. I ain't losing him *again*."

Caroline held her hands up, palms out, in surrender. "Sorry."

"You wouldn't like it anyways. It was cold, *so* cold, like that razor blade wind that comes blowin' through the fields in February. And your skin gets all prickly, like when your arm falls asleep, but not just your arm, everywhere, all over. And you can't *do* nothin' or *say* nothin'. When they're in you, they *are* you."

The knock on the door startled the girls and Lily gave off a little squeal. The door opened a couple inches and Carlos' voice whispered through the crack, "Shower if you're going to, girls." The door pulled closed again.

Lily laughed uncomfortably, but she knew it wasn't to cover up being startled by the dorm monkey.

— n · i · n · e —

Lily's eyes fluttered open. Caroline leaned over her, shaking Lily's shoulders, gently, but still hard enough to pull her from slumber.

"Make him tell me. Tommy won't tell me what he saw!" The moonlight and shadows fell on Caroline's face and made her look crazy, or evil.

Lily sat up and scooted backward, away from Caroline, as she tried to register what was going on. She scanned the darkness of the room. *Tommy?*

"Where is he?" Lily squinted at Caroline with blame, but quickly saw Caroline was scared.

"By the other hall... I'll show you."

Caroline backed away from the bed to allow Lily to get up, moving quickly to open their door quietly. Peeking both directions, Caroline indicated it was safe with the wave of her hand and disappeared into the dim hallway. Lily followed.

Walking as softly as possible, Caroline

directed Lily to walk along the wall. "The floorboards creak less."

Lily responded with nothing but a raised eyebrow and knowing smile. *Obviously, Caroline's wandered outta her room after curfew before.*

They crept past the library and the closed doors of the two teacher suites facing the library, Lily glancing at the one she'd seen Ms. Pond coming out of the night before. Caroline stopped suddenly and Lily almost ran into her.

"What?" Lily whispered behind Caroline.

Caroline pointed in front of her.

Lily followed Caroline's silent direction and found Tommy standing at the edge of the West Wing hallway, right outside what would be the lounge door on the east side and Lily wondered if they had a lounge as well.

Tommy. Lily silently called to his *inner* voice.

Help. Tommy's inner voice sounded far away and funny.

Tommy didn't turn toward them. He didn't move at all, and Lily noticed he was shaking where he stood. His expression was absolute terror, as if held by a fear far worse than the man who had killed him and held Lily captive. She gasped and rushed past Caroline.

Feeling the brush of Caroline's hand down the back of her, Lily knew the girl tried to grab her and stop her from running, but Lily didn't care. Tommy needed her.

She stopped in front of him and scrutinized his face.

Tommy crumpled to the floor as Lily heard a squeak behind her.

Lily spun to see hallways as dim as her own, a blur of motion at the far end of it masked by the shadows.

Another squeak from the stairwell behind them made Lily look back toward Caroline, who was frantically waving for her to come back.

"Go. I'm okay now." Tommy waved at her as if he could push her away. "I'm coming, but you gotta go or you'll get in trouble."

"Tommy—"

"Go…" His voice sounded tired and desperate. Lily turned and sprinted back across to the East Wing.

As they turned the corner, a woman's voice called out from the stairs, "Hello?"

Caroline pushed the door shut, holding the handle turned so it wouldn't click.

Footsteps approached their door and paused, before turning back the way they'd come from. After a few more moments, Tommy walked through the door. "She's gone."

For the hundredth time since his death, Lily wished she could hug the little boy.

"What was *that*?" Caroline asked him, leaning against her bed and exhaling deeply.

"I don't know, some teacher with purple hair. Can you believe that? Purple hair?"

"Not that. Over in the other hall. What was wrong?" Lily's brows angled downward in concern.

Tommy shuddered, and looked between the girls, fear creeping back into his expression. "Someone standing in the shadow. Just standing there. I was walking about, wandering and imagining I was on a treasure hunt, and then they were there. I heard a voice say *don't move.* And I couldn't. I couldn't move at all. No matter how hard I tried, I couldn't even turn away."

"Fucking pushers." Caroline's vulgarity stunned Lily and her mouth gaped at the girl. "Apparently, they've got one strong enough to control the dead now."

— t · e · n —

Lily and Caroline hit the bottom of the stairs just as the front door started to swing to a close behind Miz Yost. Outside, an ambulance was pulling away from the school with no lights or sirens.

Miz Yost glanced up and Lily caught her gaze.

"What was that?" Caroline sounded like an eagerly inquisitive child dancing around wrapped boxes under the Christmas tree. She stood on her tiptoes and leaned to the side, trying to see more before the door finished closing.

"There was an accident last night in the West Wing. Don't worry about it. Hurry on to class." Miz Yost strode past them, entered her office, and shut the door.

Lily watched her go, then turned back to Caroline, "Is she always so stark and honest? Almost sounds mean the way she says things."

"She's not mean. I think she used to be mad, *really* mad, but not mean. Also, she's probably had enough *little shits* listen to her thoughts over the years that she doesn't bother trying to hide things from us." Caroline snickered.

"*Little shits?*" Lily whispered the curse word and remembered the nurse thinking the exact phrase when she'd done Lily's initial exam. "Did she say that to you, too?"

"Oh god, no. But she thought it and Preston heard it. He told Tasha. Tasha told Kals. Kals told me."

"Wow… a winning round of the banana game."

"Banana game?"

"You know, everyone sits in a circle, and the first one whispers a really long silly sentence like *a bunch of yellow bananas launched on a blue boat*. Then that person whispers it to the next and the next. And when it comes 'round to the first person again, ya see how different it is…" Lily's voice drifted off as she watched Caroline's face, expecting the girl to know the game.

"Hang on. You mean *Telephone*. Same idea, different name."

Lily's face squished up in embarrassment.

"No worries. It's probably called something else up north. Or in France!" Caroline laughed to lighten the mood and Lily joined her.

"Hey what was that? Did you two see who was in the ambulance?" Kals and Odette appeared behind them on the stairs.

Lily shook her head.

"How'd you know?" Caroline looked up the stairs as the two girls completed their descent.

"Saw it from the window, but it was already closed and leaving. You don't know who?"

"Nah, Miz Yost said it was a West Winger and not to worry." Caroline turned back around and started toward class, the other three girls following her like ducks.

"I feel like we should worry *every* time it's a West Winger." Kals tapped Lily's shoulder to get her attention. "*Always.*"

Lily regarded her with wide eyes and then turned to Caroline, who shook her head lightly and made a face to indicate she thought Kals was overreacting.

Settling into their seats for first period, Lily realized the whole room was talking about the ambulance.

"I heard someone died." One of the boys spoke behind her and she spun to see who it was. Shane, the redhead with scenic memory, didn't bother to whisper. "That's why they weren't using the lights or siren. That's the protocol."

"Who?" Sam asked with disbelief.

"How do *you* know protocol?" Miko questioned and shook her head.

"It *is*. I watch a lot of cop shows and that's how they do it." Shane defended his belief without providing his source.

"How'd they die then?" Keagan looked at his roommate with one eyebrow arched high, and Lily wondered if he was questioning him or egging him on.

"Who knows, they're so weird on that side."

"Well, Odette and I got lectured yesterday about missing chef's knives." Alex nodded while he spoke, as if what he was saying was proof of something. "But I watched Odette clean those and put them away, and we told Elle that."

Odette nodded, her long mouse-brown hair tied into braids. "It's true. They were all there when we were finished after dinner."

"One of them *must* have stolen it and killed another West Winger." The redhead crossed his arms in front of him, as if vindicated.

"Woah, Shane, you didn't say murd—"

"That's enough." Kals rebuttal was cut short by Ms. Pond's entrance.

Everyone turned at her voice and immediately sat in their seats.

"Do *you* know what happened?" Sam raised his hand but spoke without waiting for her to acknowledge him.

"I know the last thing we need is people with your abilities gossiping and making shit up." She stood behind her desk, looking at her books and folder rather than the students. *Shit, I shouldn't have said that.*

Lily smiled at the teacher chiding herself, but in the face of an accident and a classroom full of busy mouths and minds, Lily figured the teacher should get a pass on the slip.

"I'll tell you what I know. But let's stick to the facts." Ms. Pond opened her folder, gave the page a once-over, sat in her chair, and exhaled before looking up to the kids. "There was indeed a death. But it was *not* a murder." She licked her lips.

Lily and Caroline turned to each other with wide eyes. From behind them, Lily heard Shane whisper under his breath. "Told ya."

"Right now they're saying suicide, but there was no note and no obvious reason. There will be an investigation."

"Who was it?" Shane asked. Lily didn't look behind her but wondered if his arm had ever come back down or if he just left it up in the air and blurted things out.

"It was Teah Kyler. Without a roommate, there was no one to know something was wrong until she didn't come down for breakfast." Ms. Pond turned to Odette. "And no, it wasn't a kitchen knife. It seems it was pills she somehow stole from the nurse's station."

That explains Miz Yost's anger.

Caroline leaned closer to Lily and whispered, "I wonder if *that* is who you saw in the library?"

Lily shrugged. "I don't think so. I can't

usually see 'em until their funeral flowers have wilted."

"Really?"

Lily nodded.

"I don't want this to degrade into an hour of speculation, so let's go ahead and work on those reading assignments for next week's unit final. I should hear nothing but pages turning for the next forty minutes." Ms. Pond surveyed the sea of faces, the curious and the worried alike.

"I'll explain it later," Lily promised, flipping her book open and shutting her mouth, afraid to get in trouble again for talking during class.

The teachers kept tight control of their classrooms that morning. Even Mr. Erne refused to open discussion about it until they had further information. When the class moved to other things, Lily gave him a wink and nodded to Caroline to let him know she knew. He nodded with approval, and then promptly covered it by asking Caroline to go to the board and solve a problem.

Lunch was the first chance they'd had to gossip again. Students who usually spread out and took over the entire room all crowded around two tables. All the seniors were over at one, talking among themselves, and the juniors were all around Lily. The tables were designed for two on a side and one at each end, but today the juniors managed to fit nine students around one table. They all had questions for her, and spoke over each other trying to be heard.

"You can see ghosts, so where's the girl?"

"And you can hear thoughts, so what are the

teachers hiding from us?"

"I can't yet, though." Lily addressed the ghost issue again and looked at her roommate. "I was telling Caroline earlier, I can't see no ghosts until they've been dead about a week. Clara—" Lily paused and then chose to lie about the source rather than discuss her conversations with another ghost. "Meemaw says it's so's people can get over the first bit of ugly mourning before their loved ones saw their trauma."

"What's a meemaw?" Alex leaned on the table and turned his attention from Caroline to Lily.

"Um, my grandmother. That what we call our grandmothers." Lily was afraid her roots were going to shun her in this crowd.

"Ah okay. Mine is Nana. I guess everyone has a nickname for them." Alex sat back again, paying more attention to Caroline than to Lily, and Lily was glad for both his attention and his acceptance of her meemaw.

Lily looked over at Kals and addressed her question, "The teachers are all trying really hard to not think about it."

"They can do that? Block you?"

"It's not that so much as I usually hear extreme emotions, like love and hate. Sadness is pretty strong, too, but I'm not sure any of them are necessarily sad right now. Just kind of in shock. So, their minds are…" Lily looked around the table and wondered how many of them worried about her digging into their minds. "And I was told I'm not supposed to snoop in people's minds without permission. Like a rule for me and people like me. But that I can practice in class and stuff when it's a controlled situation."

Lily saw both Odette and Keagan relax at the idea she wasn't randomly reading their minds. Kals slumped, obviously disappointed at Lily's answer and abilities.

"You can see trauma, right? What if we went up there?" Lily tried to deflect it to Kals' abilities.

"Nah, I gotta touch the person. Wouldn't do me any good to go up there in the room. Though you know, I never thought about it until now, but I bet that would be damn handy in a coroner's office."

"*Ewww* really, Kals? Touching dead people?" Miko made a face of disgust.

"You *hear* them, how's it any different?"

"I hear what they want me to hear. I'm not probing into their final minutes."

Caroline looked wounded at Miko's reaction. "But I do that, too. If I'm where they died, I can see it…"

Miko looked at Caroline's large brown eyes and bit her lip. "I'm sorry. I didn't mean…"

"It's okay."

"Wait, what if *you* went up there?" Kals asked Caroline with a mischievous look on her face.

"I'd rather not see that."

Kals slumped back and blew her auburn bangs out of her way in exasperation.

"What is going on out here?" Elle was suddenly standing in the doorway of the kitchen scrutinizing the group of them huddled together and the empty tables throughout the dining hall.

Lily waited, wondering which of them would say something. No one did.

"That's what I thought. Now spread out and finish your lunch. I need those dishes." Elle disappeared back into the kitchen.

The other students grabbed their trays and returned to their normal seats, spread out across three tables. The seniors followed suit and spread among four, sitting in smaller groups. There were still a lot of empty tables, and Lily imagined the room full—back when it was loaded with boys after the war, rather than just a handful of kids with bizarre abilities. She thought about the countless meals that had happened in the room while she picked at her salad.

A whole bowl of lettuce as a meal? Really? Lily had thought that behavior was saved for California and television. She pulled the cauliflower and tomatoes free and popped them in her mouth. *Salad is taking already gross lettuce and making it soggy with milk syrup.* Lily's abject hatred of ranch dressing spread across condiments and made her avoid mayonnaise on sandwiches.

After lunch, the dean of students met them at the bottom of the stairs. "Bathroom breaks if you need, but please head to the Assembly room rather than your next class."

They walked past her up the stairs, Lily already used to Caroline's preference for the upstairs bathroom. Halfway up the stairs, they heard the dean repeat her instructions for the next chunk of students who approached the stairs.

Back down in the Assembly room, Lily finally saw all the East Wing students in one group, not spread out like in the cafeteria. The students filed into chairs set up in neat rows, like when Pastor Jacob put the folding chairs outside for weddings. The teachers, dean, and some man Lily hadn't met yet were at the front of the room. They mostly sat at one of the two tables there. The strange man stood behind the podium between the tables, his bald head shined under the florescent lights and judging by his rimless glasses and age, Lily assumed him to be the headmaster. After several minutes of settling whispers and fidgeting, the man cleared his throat and the room quieted immediately.

"Good afternoon, students." He found Lily May in the front row next to Caroline and nodded to her. "I'm Headmaster Landry." Turning back to the rest of the students, he continued. "We have had a unfortunate tragedy in the West Wing. One of our students, a bright, *promising* girl, has chosen to take her own life. We'll be interviewing all the seniors, and any juniors who knew Teah…" He looked across the two rows of juniors. Lily peripherally saw most of them shrug, and noted Sam nodded with reverence and respect. *He must have known her, or CJ did and therefore he was included.*

"After assembly, we're going to have an afternoon of study in the library. Everyone. We'll take students one at a time to talk to them regarding Teah. The rest of you will study quietly. If you need help with any classes, this is your chance to get aid from your teachers, as they'll be in their classrooms for both tutoring and counseling should you feel you need to talk to someone. If you need neither and are somehow caught up on homework, read a book."

He raised an eyebrow and Lily couldn't tell who he was aiming his gaze at, but she guessed someone was smart enough to breeze through their homework on a regular enough basis that it was known.

"This was a horrible accident that had nothing to do with anyone or anything here, and no one else is in danger. We'd like to stress that to all of you. This wasn't tied to her abilities at all. The best thing we can do is get back to the business of learning and training, and pray for her family." He put his hands flat on the podium, as if to signal he was done. "Are there any questions?"

From the back row of seniors, Lily heard the whispered question, "Has Jezzy been found?"

Being grounded to the library because of the tragedy offered Lily an opportunity to catch up on almost all of the back work she'd been assigned. Ms. Pond sat at the librarian desk, rather than in her classroom downstairs, and watched the students over the pages of a novel. Looking up occasionally, she kept a tight reign on the chatter—the only noises in the room were the grandfather clock and the turning of pages.

"It's just their attempt to keep us calm. The library is a *soothing* room. Cozy." Miko had proffered as they filed in and found seats.

Kals had raised an eyebrow at her. "And to stop the gossiping."

Ms. Pond had separated everyone into smaller groups at tables, as if to ensure Kals' theory. Alyssa had been seated with Lily, and Lily found it difficult to not *feel* the girl's mean glances and judgmental stares. She really didn't understand why Alyssa was so angry.

Lily had to think for a moment, but then

remembered Alyssa's ability was to touch items and know where the person was. *Maybe her abilities showed her something she never got over?* Lily suggested to Tommy as they spoke silently, using their *inner* voices.

Or maybe she's just mean like my mamma. Tommy scowled at Alyssa and wandered over to Caroline's table.

Closing her history book, the final worksheet finished, Lily stood and approached the librarian desk. "May I please go to the bathroom?"

Ms. Pond looked up over the edge of her glasses at Lily. "Yes, Lily. And in the future, you do not have to ask when in *here*. The library is open study."

"Okay, ma'am. Thank you."

Lily paused at the table next to hers and leaned down to Odette. "I'll be right back. I need a potty break."

Odette nodded and returned her attention on the book in front of her. As she looked down, her eyes disappear beneath her long bangs, and Lily imagined the girl could nap like that and no one would ever know.

In the foyer outside the library, Lily turned to the right to go to the larger, second floor bathroom Caroline seemed to prefer. The janitor, or so she assumed from the garbage can and supplies on his wheeled cart, stood at the end of the West Wing and watched her. She felt a chill run up her spine and hurried into the lavatory.

While the downstairs bathroom had stalls and sinks like any number of public restrooms Lily had been in, the second floor bathroom was huge, with twice as many amenities as the one below, and a shower area in the back. At the end of the stalls, a tiled wall jutted out halfway across the room, acting as a barrier between toilets and showers. Around the other side of it, was a fully tiled room with over a dozen showerheads along the four walls, each with a small bench below and hooks above for towels and robes, as well as a curtain you could pull around you like a tiny little enclosure to feign privacy—much like the hospital beds she'd seen back home.

The slightest noises echoed off the clean white tiles, but Lily had noticed if there were students showering, the water damped the air and there was no echo. However, at the moment, in the middle of the day, her every footstep resounded. The click of the lock on the stall door repeated in the empty air as she twisted it. And even her urine stream seemed to have a shadow of sound in the empty room. She washed and dried her hands, noting even the mechanics of the cloth towel dispenser was loud in the quiet, as it moved her used portion to the back to provide a clean section for the next person.

Back in the hall, the subtle noises of the school filled in again and made the vastness of everything warmer, more comfortable. For a moment.

I remember another pencil like this. Dark like this. Got it from that girl who stopped fighting and fell limp. She didn't need it no more.

Lily spun her head toward the voice and saw the janitor still standing at the edge of the West Wing.

The girl who...?

Limp?

Did he...

Lily watched in horror as he scrubbed something black onto his fingers, smiled at the dusty coating, and then wiped it across his pants leg, smearing it into a stain from countless previous applications.

The river was dried up. Dead like the girl. He looked up at Lily and cocked his head. *Well that one looks just like the girl with the warm throat.*

Lily's eyes widened in horror and she spun to her left to rush into the safety of the library. She ran right into Mr. Erne coming from his suite.

"*Oof*, Lily." He caught her and took a step backward to keep his balance.

"Mr. Erne..." Fear moved her and she walked *at* him, forcing him to continue backward. She matched his stride, as she herded him toward the short hallway of male teacher's suites. She watched the West Wing until she was out of sight of it and then turned to look at Mr. Erne.

"Lily?"

"Mr. Erne, that man. That man is a killer. I *think*. I think he's a killer. I think he killed a girl. Maybe two. Or at least hurt them real, real bad." She spoke with a rapid-fire cadence, which punctuated her panic. "His thoughts... His thoughts are cruel but satisfied, like it were fun or pleasing to hurt them girls. So horrible. So close to the surface. So loud—"

"Calm down, Lily." Mr. Erne grabbed her by the shoulders and stared into her eyes. "Lily?" He waited for her focus to come back to him rather than be locked on the janitor.

"But Mr. Erne—"

"It's okay, Lily. I promise." He released her shoulders, and she saw his eyes soften. "Go ahead, listen to my insides, I'd never lie to you."

Lily swallowed. "I want to believe you, but his thoughts. I heard that man's thoughts."

"And they were likely exactly what you heard. But it's not a memory to him, it's almost like something he watched on television and not real."

"So he didn't...?"

"No, unfortunately, he did. But that was a long time ago and he's here now. He's been treated and medicated and done his time. He's not dangerous anymore. Not a threat." Mr. Erne's thoughts matched his words and Lily relaxed a little. "He's not nearly as much a threat

PASSAGES

as some students we've had come through the West Wing. That is far more hazardous to you. I understand you're new, and curious, but don't go looking. You stay out of the West Wing, alright?"

Lily nodded and wondered if there were any dangerous children over there *now*, or if it was just a blanket warning.

He knocked on the door next to them, marked with a brass number four centered below a peephole. "This is me. Any time you need to see me, to talk or just ask questions, you can find me in my classroom or here. Any time. And if you want to join Caroline and I on Sunday for our floor picnics you can." His smile was soft and reassuring.

Lily nodded, feeling silly for making a fuss. "Could I maybe go to church on Sundays?"

"Oh, I don't think any of the other students do. But Miss Mac does, I'll talk to her and see what we can work out, okay?"

Lily May nodded at him, her heart feeling better even if her mind was still leery of the janitor's past and possibilities.

"You'll wear shoes to church, right?" His gaze fell to her bare feet and Lily giggled.

"Of course." He gave her a smile and a nod. "I'll let you know. Now you head on back to—are you all still in the library?"

"Yes, sir."

"Well then head on back there, Little Lady."

— t·h·i·r·t·e·e·n —

At the very end of catching up on the current units of each of her classes, Lily returned to the library after dinner. While she knew her new friends were right down the hall in the lounge, the heavy closed door of the library was an effective sound barrier, and she was once again in the presence of nothing but her studies and the ticking of the grandfather clock. The steady sounds of the rhythmic pendulum seemed to help Lily keep cadence with her work. The hourly chimes were a low, almost muted, timbre, and Lily wondered if it was somehow adjusted for use in the library, where things are *expected* to be quiet. On the hour, it once again punctuated the pattern and she glanced up to verify the time—eight o'clock. She turned back to her work. She only had one sheet left to do for science and it wasn't due until Friday.

Plenty of time.

She packed up her books and papers, and pushed her chair back to stand. The scrape of the heavy wooden chair against the hardwood floor *almost* covered the gasp from the direction of the librarian's desk.

Lily froze.

She knew she heard it but for some reason she felt anxiety at checking it out, and suddenly couldn't distinguish if the uncomfortable feeling was hers or the other person's. Slowly, she turned toward the back of the room.

The strawberry blonde vision stood behind the desk, staring at Lily, with the same look of fear on her face she'd had the other day.

"It's okay," Lily tried to reassure her. "I won't hurt you."

The girl took a step back, as Lily heard the heavy door to the foyer open behind her. Lily heard unassuming casual footsteps enter the library and move to the left, before stopping and coming back toward the center where Lily stood. In response, the girl turned and fled into the small office next to the librarian's desk.

"Who was that?"

Lily turned to see a female version of Sam, standing several inches taller than he was, but with the same brown eyes and spikey short hair—CJ. She'd never met her, but it was easy to deduce this was Sam's older sister. They could almost be twins.

"Wait, you saw her?" Lily narrowed her eyes at CJ's face with anticipation.

"Of course I did. She wasn't very stealthy."

"I thought she was a ghost." Lily ran through the powers she'd been told everyone had, trying to remember what exactly CJ's gifts were.

"Ghosts? Oh hell no. I don't play that game."

Oh yeah, Lily remembered, *astral—she can leave her body behind and go floating around.* Lily smiled at the suddenly funny idea of her papa's reaction to the students here. *Talk like this would have made Papa afraid… or angry.*

"She was real." CJ pulled Lily from her musings with an expression meant to question Lily's strange grin. "Real, and really not where she should be. You may want to remind your little friend we're not allowed back there."

Lily nodded and CJ turned away from her and moved toward the left side, where her footsteps had originally wandered. Lily watched CJ go and thought again how very alike she and Sam looked, except CJ was paler. Much paler. Almost as if her colors were off. Or muddy.

Oh noooo.

Lily scooped up her homework and ran from the room, bursting into the lounge in a panic. Finding Caroline with Sam and Alex, playing some board game that included shark fins and small boats, she approached the table and dropped into an empty chair.

"Caroline." She tried to whisper, but excitement and fear made it come out in a hoarse demand. "I need to talk to you about CJ."

"What about her?" Sam leaned forward, and Lily realized her whisper had failed.

"Her colors." Lily looked around the room and tried to calm down her breathing and heartbeat. "Her colors are all muddy."

"Her colors?" Alex raised an eyebrow at Lily.

"So?" Sam shrugged.

"You don't understand!" Lily's voice was higher and louder than she'd expected and a girl stood from the couch to turn and look at them with concern.

Tommy, sitting next to the couch, turned toward her as well. *What's wrong?*

The girl from the couch, tall and lean with a long caramel colored ponytail in her hair and PJ pants poking out from under an oversized t-shirt, approached the table. "Everything alright?"

Caroline held up a hand and nodded to the girl. Turning to Lily, she explained, "This is Tasha. She's okay and she can calm you down."

"She can *what*? I'm not *not* calm. I'm—" Lily turned back to Sam. "CJ's colors are bad. Like she's going to die."

Sam sat straight up, pulling away from the table with a look of horror. Alex and Caroline followed with expressions of concern and confusion rather than fear. Tasha simply squatted down next to Lily's chair and put both her hands on Lily's leg.

"Lily is it?"

Lily felt a rush of warmth spread from Tasha's hands. The sensation travelled to Lily's extremities and up her spine. It wasn't painful or even startling, but more like an all over hug. Lily felt her shoulders drop, as the tension released and her muscles relaxed.

"What did you…?" Lily looked at the girl.

"It's what I do. I can calm people down." Tasha smiled and moved one hand to Lily's back. "Now what's going on? What were you saying about CJ?"

"Her colors are muddy."

"Yes, but what does that *mean*?"

Lily's eyes danced from Tasha to the rest of the group and it dawned on her, she'd never told them about *that* gift—what the dean had called *aura sensing*. They only knew about hearing and speaking to the living and the dead. She took a deep breath and prepared for their reaction.

"Ever since I was little, maybe even before I could hear what people was thinking, I could tell when they was gonna pass. It was like their colors got all… muddy. Not a glow like the dean tried to say *auras* are, but just that they're like…" Lily pulled the corner of her lower lip into her mouth to chew at it while she thought. "I guess like they were *faded*? Been through the wash and hung out to dry in the hot sun too many times, like old jeans."

"And CJ's colors were like this?" Tasha *asked* Lily but was watching Sam.

Lily nodded and whispered, "Yes."

"Is it always death? It's not sickness like—" Tasha looked around the room for a moment. "Doesn't one of you *see* sickness?"

"That's me." Alex raised his hand briefly.

"Could it be like that? Just that she's sick?" Tasha's voice was almost as calming as her touch, but while one was her ability, the other was simply her natural demeanor.

"It never has been…" Lily felt like she was going to cry, as she turned to Sam. "I'm sorry. I'm so, so sorry."

"Maybe it's something I can see. Maybe we can stop it." Alex proffered, his eyes darting between Sam and Lily.

"Nah, it's okay." Sam waved off the panic at the table as he sat back. "If Lily sees death, then it's death."

Lily couldn't believe how well he was taking it, and could hear the rush of concern in the heads around her—not for CJ, but rather for Sam's cavalier attitude toward his sister's impending doom.

Sam's eyes grew wider as he took in the table of faces. "Oh hey, no. Wait guys. I didn't mean—" He laughed a sharp uncomfortable sounding laugh. "She *already* died. It's all good."

"She what?" Alex regarded his roommate like he was a stranger.

"Oh yeah, back when we were little." Sam checked around the room. "Where is she? Wasn't she just in here?"

"She's in the library. I saw her in the library." Lily whispered the words, stunned almost silent by the news of CJ's previous death.

"Okay. I just didn't wanna get biffed in the back of the head for talking about her, so don't be going and telling her either." He spoke to the table but was looking at Tasha, who nodded in response. "CJ's heart stopped when she was getting her tonsils taken out. Heck of a way to find out you have an allergy to sedation, and a bad enough reaction that they immediately marked *my* chart just to be sure. But they did whatever it is they do and brought her back. But she was technically, *clinically*, dead for almost three minutes. So yes, she died."

Lily felt better, but she wasn't sure if it was due to Tasha's touch or Sam's explanation. She tried to think back to other people she'd seen go muddy.

"Matter of fact," Sam continued. "She used to be a remote viewer like me. It wasn't until *after* she died that her ability changed to astral viewing, or as she calls it, *leveling up*." He grinned and fiddled with the game board pieces in front of him.

Lily exhaled again, slowly, and relaxed. *Must be what I saw.* She glanced over at Tommy, still sitting on the floor watching television with the older kids. He turned and smiled at her.

It was nothing, Tommy. No worries. She answered his question finally, but tried to remember if *his* colors had been muddy after he died the first time.

— f·o·u·r·t·e·e·n —

In the aftermath of the girl's suicide, each teacher took time to talk to the students about depression and anxiety. In their own ways, they tried to implore over and over how important it was to reach out—both if you needed help, or if you thought someone else did.

"It never hurts to be wrong, but someone can get hurt if you do nothing." Mr. Erne had told Lily, after she explained muddy colors to him.

"Back home, ain't no one wanted me in their head, and they sure didn't want me mussin' with their plans." Lily shook her head, remembering how her papa had run and saved Mrs. Miller from hanging herself when Lily told him.

Mr. Erne suggested they were upset because they couldn't see an alternative and didn't *want* her help, but assured her it was still always best to tell someone. *Always.*

In a strange way, McMillan Hall mourned a student many of them had never met by talking about what she'd done and promising to always be there for each other. They talked about it a lot the first few days, and then it drifted as things do, and finally, life seemed to normal out again. Or as normal as a school of psychically gifted children could get.

There was no more spotting of students where they shouldn't be in the library, the ghosts in the hall had settled down and become accustomed to the new student, and even the abilities themselves started to feel as if everyone in the world could do these things.

But the homework never stopped. So close to the end of the year, it felt like the teachers were piling up both bookwork and what they called *skill studies*.

In social studies they discussed how to use your gifts to help those in need. Unlike in Mr. Erne's class—where they concentrated on working for and with *authorities*—Mr. Pence's was about working with *victims*. Other than the strange conversations in classes where teachers could point out a use or purpose for an ability in the field, it felt just like a school. Albeit a posh, private, tucked away in the middle of nowhere school.

Lily was far from home. And while her surroundings were exciting and wonderful, she was homesick for her family. She was pleased to learn they were allowed to call home any time they wanted. They simply needed to tell a teacher

who could put them in an office or classroom—
somewhere private—and give them access to
the landlines. The other kids laughed that there
still were landlines, a couple of them lamenting
about the no cellphone rule, but Lily was more
than happy to use an old-school telephone. She
took the opportunity to call home every couple of
days, usually after dinner. She learned Meemaw
was working on a quilt for the Mason's new baby,
and Mamma was busy baking for the church
bazaar. They were planning on coming to visit in
a couple weeks, and most of the calls were asking
about her friends and classes and what kinds of
things she might miss from home that they could
bring with her. She requested a huckleberry pie.

During the first weekend, she'd been taken
clothes shopping by Mrs. Duran and was given a
list of suggestions and several hundred dollars.
Lily had no idea how to spend that much
money, expecting they were going to Wal-Mart
or something similar. Instead, she was taken
to an outlet mall and the dean helped her with
outfits, under garments, and even accessories.
She brought her to a shoe store that sold nothing
but shoes, and Lily promised to wear at least
flip-flops or sandals, but the dean smiled and
assured her she could be barefoot for classes,
but not for lunch or PE. Once they'd gotten her
wardrobe in order, Mrs. Duran asked Lily if
she was interested in piercing her ears like the

other kids, but Lily blanched at the idea.

Returning to her dorm with a new wardrobe, her old clothes seemed frumpy. While the new clothes weren't in any *fancy* style she wasn't used to—she stuck to dresses and simple blouses—but they were made of *nicer* materials and had cleaner, stylish stitching. Lily packed all her old clothes, except her favorite white dress, back into the brown suitcase. She hoped if they were out of sight, the strangeness of it all wouldn't sting as much.

By the second Sunday, she was going to church with Miss Mac and then coming back to join Caroline and her father for their floor picnics. She learned how he would do this when Caroline was younger to appease the little girl who wanted to go outside even when it was raining. He didn't realize it for a while, but it was because there was a ghost in their house Caroline didn't like, so she always wanted to be outside, away from it. Because the ghost had lived in their home but not died there, there was no *ghost blood* to let Mr. Erne know. Caroline's first paranormal conversation with her father was about *that* ghost, and learning what her father could do made her feel so much closer to normal, or at least okay for *not* being normal.

Once Lily was caught up with the units and on track with the rest of the students, she took the quizzes and tests with the rest of them, and learned a strange tidbit no one had mentioned. Ms. Pond handed out tests wearing white gloves. Lily leaned over to Caroline and then chose to ask the teacher herself, rather than have Ms. Pond presume she and Caroline were discussing the test. As it turned out, *all* the teachers wore gloves when handling quizzes or tests, so *touchers* couldn't feel the answers.

Clever, Lily thought, and wondered what other precautions teachers had taken to protect or prevent the talented from cheating.

Lily spent her time on the duty roster, gathering laundry and bringing it down to Ava, and then cleaning up with Elle in the kitchen. She wasn't alone in the kitchen however, as the gardener, Mr. Young, was also helping the girls.

"Warren, please." He said, his voice as soft as his eyes appeared to be.

Warren, not Mister, just like Caroline said.

Lily nodded. "Okay, Warren."

She noticed the old scars of long ago burned flesh on his hands, but didn't ask about it. He was sweet and pleasant to be around, always smiling at the children, and she didn't want to tarnish how she felt about him.

He grinned. "When it rains all day, like today and tomorrow will, I just come inside and make myself useful."

"And we adore you for it." Elle told him as she tossed him a dishtowel. He caught it with a smile and helped Lily with the dinner mess.

Everything felt right, and by the beginning of the third week, the strangest thing in Lily's life was watching Miko and Tommy.

Because Miko could hear Tommy but not *see* him, and because Lily knew exactly who it was, she had reassured Miko he was kind and safe. And then they used the situation to help Miko get better with her skills. While Lily was reading on her bed, she watched peripherally as Miko would sit in a chair and Tommy would move around her and talk, then Miko would try and pinpoint where he was. Caroline called it Ghostie Polo, and while Lily didn't get it at first, when Caroline explained the game Marco Polo, Lily agreed it was quite similar.

On occasion, Miko wouldn't quite catch where Tommy's voice was coming from and would beg Caroline or Lily for a clue. Lily always shook her head—though she *wanted* to help, she knew it wouldn't do Miko any good to cheat. Caroline, on the other hand, couldn't help but look directly at Tommy and thereby give Miko the directional clue she was after.

Miko and Tommy had been playing their nightly game for over an hour, Miko having an extraordinarily difficult time that night. Tommy sat on the bed next to Lily and slumped, while Miko took her glasses off to wipe them with her shirt.

"It's not fair, you know that, right?" Miko spoke softly but there was an edge to her voice. "Both of you can hear him *and* see him, but I'm like some mutant who can't even get her powers right."

"Don't be silly. Ya just hafta figure out why yours is different." Lily assured her from over the edge of her history book.

"That's what everyone sa—" Miko had glanced up to answer Lily and instead froze midsentence. She squinted, her glasses still in her hands. "What is that next to you?"

Lily watched Miko's eyebrows knit tightly together and fear begin to crawl into her expression. Lily looked around frantically, but saw nothing other than Tommy.

Tommy?

"Oh my goodness, Miko. Can you *see* Tommy?" Lily dropped her book to the bed and sat up. She reached forward and put her hands on either side of Tommy, wishing as usual she could grab him, hold him, or hug him. "This is where Tommy is, Miko. He's 'tween my hands."

"Oh my god, oh my god, oh my god." Miko jumped up from the chair and dove toward the bed, stopping in front of Tommy and waving her hand around. He made a face when her forearm went through him. "This is you? This is really you? Why can I—" She looked down to the glasses in her hands.

Caroline, having watched the whole thing with fascination, burst into laughter on her bed. "Your glasses *fix* your vision!"

"What do you see?" Lily waved at Caroline to stop, but the girl just kept giggling, finding something about the situation far funnier than Lily thought.

"A weird blur, like someone scribbled across the air with an eraser."

"Do you see his shirt? What color is his shirt?"

"I see a red blur, but I don't see the lines. I can't even make out the details of his face, just a round blur."

Lily thought for a moment. "Okay, Miko. Close your eyes."

"Why?" Miko stood upright, glasses still in her hand, and looked at Lily.

"So's he can move an' we can see if you can find him." Lily winked at Tommy to indicate the plan.

"Ohhh…" Miko rushed back to the chair and sat down, then she closed and covered her eyes. "Okay."

Tommy moved over by Caroline's dresser and opened his mouth to talk, but Lily hushed him with a finger to her lips and a quick shake of her head.

"Okay, Miko. Open your eyes and see if ya can find him."

Miko opened her eyes and turned to Lily, scanning her bed and side of the room. She turned to Caroline, still snickering, and surveyed her side of the room. She shrugged and turned around toward the door, taking a step back as she gasped and covered her mouth.

"Is that you? Are you by the dresser?"

Tommy nodded, which sent Caroline into another fit of laughter. "She can't see you nodding, Tommy. No details, Tommy, you're just a blur remember?"

Tommy regarded Caroline with a pinched expression, then turned to Miko and waves his arms up and down as if he were helping an airplane pull up to the gate.

"Oh my god, it *is* you! Do it again!" Miko didn't bother to sit back down and simply shut her eyes where she stood. She waited several moments as Lily told Tommy to move. When Miko opened her eyes again, she found him. She had to squint, but she could find him now that she knew what to look for.

They did it several more times, then tried it in both brighter light with the overhead on, and in the dimmer light of the hallway curfew sconces. Miko was almost crying with joy by the time curfew was called.

"He's not clear, but I can see him. I can *see* him." She grinned wide and put her glasses on, her mouth changing immediately to a disappointed slack jaw. "And now he's gone."

Miko took her glasses off and Tommy walked her to her room, stating he was going to hang with her a little longer.

Lily felt a pang of jealousy. Tommy had been hers alone for so long and now she was sharing him with Caroline *and* Miko. He was delighted, seeming happier than he'd ever been while alive. He was accepted for what he was here, just like Lily, and while she knew she should be happy for Tommy, she still sometimes missed the quiet of their secret life.

— f · i · f · t · e · e · n —

Lily got back from her shower to find Tommy and Caroline talking in hushed whispers.

"What do you mean, there's passageways?" Caroline's face was twisted into disbelief. "I've been here for five years, and I've never even heard a rumor of—"

"There are!" Tommy's ghost voice squeaked with determination.

"What's going on?" Lily put her bathroom caddy on the floor next to her dresser and turned to the two of them.

"I was tryin' to find the girl. The one what trapped me in the hall." Tommy's lip curled up as if he were about to have a tantrum.

"Oh, the West Winger? I forgot about that." Lily felt bad, but acclimating to her new world had pushed the incident from her mind as it filled with so many other details.

"I didn't." He glanced from her to Caroline and back. "So I've been looking for her and I found a gap in the wall. Then I found another gap. And then I realized I could walk around in there, but not like a normal old building with a wide hollow in the wall, this felt... it's like it's there on purpose. But I found them walking *through* the wall. I can't find the real entrance, you know, for *people*."

"It *is* an old building. Could be anything from maintenance access to speakeasy hiding spots," Caroline suggested.

"Speakeasy?" Lily arched an eyebrow at Caroline.

"Yeah, during prohibit—"

"No no, I know what it is, it's just... here? In the middle of nowhere Pennsylvania?"

Caroline shrugged. "Would be cool though, wouldn't it?"

Lily smiled and acquiesced to the notion. She turned to Tommy, "Can you show us where?"

He nodded and headed for the door. Lily checked the time on the small alarm clock on the dresser, hemming as she noted the time. "We really shouldn't."

"You're right," Caroline agreed. "Not right now, anyway. We have to wait. They do the shower call, then true curfew, then a walk-through about eleven. After that we're in the clear... if we're quiet."

"Are you sure?"

Caroline nodded, "Yeah, I used to get in trouble all the time because I'd sneak out of dad's suite and go get snacks in the kitchen."

"So you stopped?"

"Nah... Eventually got really good at it." Her grin was full of innocent pride.

"Okay then, we wait." Lily hopped onto her bed and looked at her history book briefly before deciding she had better ways to wait.

Caroline crawled onto Lily's bed with her and spent the next hour whispering to her about the things she'd seen and heard in the school over the years. The rumors passed around by students with abilities to pull information. The teenage drama.

Lily wasn't stunned to learn their math teacher, Ms. Hunt, had recently had a bad breakup. Lily had heard as much. And she wasn't necessarily surprised to find out the ex-boyfriend was Mr. Pence. What stunned her was the reasoning, which had been probed out by Drake, the senior with telepathy.

"Apparently, Mr. Pence's telepathy heard something he wasn't supposed to. And remember, Ms. Hunt doesn't have any abilities and can only block her thoughts if she concentrates on doing it. When she's relaxed, well, she's an open book. And according to Drake, she was thinking about her ex-boyfriend while—" Caroline glanced at Tommy, "While her and Mr. Pence were, um, *doing the deed.*"

Lily's eyes and mouth were a comical

expression of shock, which immediately crumbled both of them into giggles. "Oh how awful." She felt bad for Ms. Hunt, but then again, for Mr. Pence. "I don't know which one I feel worse for…"

Agitated for being ignored for gossip, Tommy left the room for a while. Upon returning, he declared everyone was in their rooms and it was time. When asked where he had gone, he simply shrugged.

Lily knew it was a tantrum, he was still a little boy and his feelings were hurt. "Sorry," she whispered. "Lead the way."

"It surrounds the library. So we should start there." Tommy walked through the door, but waited for them to open it and enter the dim corridor.

"The library?" Lily shook her head, and tried to remember what book she had read with secret passages in the library. It seemed so familiar, but she couldn't place it.

"For real?" Caroline covered her mouth to keep the snicker in. "Let me guess, we have to move a book or slide a bookcase?"

Tommy shrugged. "There was food wrappers and a pillow and a blanket in there. Someone was hiding in there."

"Maybe the janitor? He's a bad man." Lily remembered her run in with him between the bathroom and library.

"What do you mean a bad man?" Caroline stopped her sneaking and turned to Lily.

Lily shushed her and continued to the library, pulling the door open so they could slip inside. Once the door was safely closed, she turned to Caroline. "I can never hear anything when I'm in here, so no one should hear us now."

"The janitor?" Caroline pushed the subject.

"He did some really bad things. But your papa said it was a long time ago and he's better now. Medicated."

Caroline pursed her lips and thought for a moment. "He has an apartment in the basement, no real need for a pillow and blanket in the wall. Unless there's a way from the basement up to here through the walls. I mean, there's the elevator…"

"Tommy? Does it go around to the other side of the linen access? The little hall next to the library by the elevator?"

He shrugged. "I don't think so. Just this side of it, by the books, and over there." He pointed to the other side of the library.

Lily looked around them. "Well if there's a doorway or secret latch or something, it won't be in the middle, so I guess we just check along the edge, right?"

Caroline turned to the left. "I'll do this side."

Almost an hour later, having done a cursory check of every shelf and each book on them running down the two outside walls, they met at the grandfather clock at the front of the room.

"Anything?" Caroline questioned.

Lily shook her head, realizing she didn't really think it would be that simple. This wasn't a movie or a book, it was a school. An old school with secrets. She glanced around as the clock struck midnight. "Where's Tommy?"

Caroline scanned the aisles and shrugged. "There's nothing in here. Should we check the basement?"

Lily winced. She didn't like the idea of being near the janitor again. "Not tonight. It's late and I'm tired. Can we do it tomorrow?"

Caroline nodded, and they slipped from the library, crept down the hall and back to their room. As she was shutting the door, Lily noticed Miko's door across the hall was open. From inside she heard Tommy's voice.

"The dead know more than the living do..."

Lily remembered when Tommy had told her the same thing. And when he'd later told her she couldn't tell the detective because it was a secret he didn't want her sharing. But here he was telling Miko.

Lily smiled, knowing Tommy was truly happy and felt safe here, and shut her door for the night.

The following night, careful to duck below the peephole in Carlos' door and go slowly so the floor wouldn't squeak, Caroline and Lily snuck down the forbidden back steps. The classroom wing was separate from the main center of the building where the library was, so they only gave each room a cursory examination—checking shelving and closets for where *they* would hide an entrance. Moving past the office, they entered the dining hall, knowing it was directly below the library where the hidden passages were on the second floor.

There didn't seem to be any secrets available in the cafeteria. The outer walls had windows, unlike the upper floor, as well as doors on either side leading to the courtyards. The kitchen was more closed in and at least offered hiding spots in the pantry, but nothing budged, nothing moved, nothing revealed itself. They both studied the elevator for a long minute before shaking their heads at each other in unison.

"It'll make noise, won't it?" Lily questioned in a whisper.

Caroline nodded. "Yeah, it's not the quietest thing. It's not meant for luxury, just for staff and service. You haven't been down there yet, have you? The linen access or the elevator? The laundry room?"

"I was in the laundry room back on the first day. Ava showed me where it was when she headed down there to switch the clothes from washers to dryers. Is the elevator and this little stairway the only way down there?"

"No, the back stairs in either wing goes all the way to the basement. Remember, on the west side there's tunnels for PE and the headmaster's cottage."

"And they go down and connect to the laundry?"

"Sorta. I'll show you. But let's finish checking this floor first." Caroline slipped silently through the swinging kitchen door.

In the main hall she looked left and right and then turned back to Lily. "Which one do you want to check first? Office or Nurse?"

Lily didn't think they should go in either of those locations, not out of fear, but out of a healthy respect she'd been raised with. Those were private offices, not open classrooms and a kitchen. It felt weird and wrong, and if she didn't choose then maybe she wouldn't have guilt.

"You choose." She told Caroline.

Caroline turned to the right and walked behind the nurse's desk. She turned the knob for the office, slowly, prepared to push it gently to keep things quiet, but the door didn't open. She let go, as she stood upright.

"Locked." She tried again as if something would have changed, and shook her head when nothing did. "That's unusual. It's never locked."

"But that girl got ahold of pills 'member?"

"*Ohhhh* crap."

Lily watched Caroline's expression as she recalled the *way* the West Wing girl had killed herself several weeks beforehand.

"It's probably been locked ever since. Though the cabinets inside have locks on them, too. Must just be precaution." Caroline nodded as if confirming a discussion.

"Or guilt."

Caroline turned to Lily and squinted at her. "Guilt? For what?"

"I think Miz Yost was feeling responsible that morning for the girl using drugs from *her* office."

"Oh wow… I hadn't even thought of that. I saw her a couple days ago, too, and she seemed a bit off. Maybe she should talk to Mr. Pence about that."

"Maybe *we* should tell Mr. Pence."

"Maybe…" Caroline walked past Lily and

went back the other direction in the main hall, stopping at Miss Mac's desk. Caroline sighed heavily as she went behind it and opened the office door, and Lily realized even Caroline felt dirty for snooping in the office.

Locked files and desk drawers, a particularly boring supply closet, and no secret entrance after fifteen minutes, left the girls standing at the doorway wondering the same thing Tommy was. Where was the entrance?

"We must have missed something." Lily suggested.

"Unless it's in the basement."

Lily shuddered. She'd never been a fan of basements and wasn't looking forward to her duties in the well-lit laundry room, which she had only gotten out of because her bruised ribs gave her a *no lifting* written excuse from Miz Yost. "Tomorrow maybe? It's late."

"Okay. And tomorrow, we tell Tommy to come with. It would be much quicker if he just went through all the walls and checked internally at the same time."

Lily felt uncomfortable at Caroline's desire to *use* Tommy, but understood the validity of what she was saying. He'd been spending a lot of time with Miko, helping her get better at seeing him and the other ghosts in the wing without her glasses. While Lily didn't mind, she did miss his company.

"I'll see what I can do." Lily and Caroline slipped once more through the hallways and back stairs, up to their room, and into bed without anyone being the wiser. Lily was impressed with Caroline's skills and wondered if the girl had made a game out of not getting caught when she was younger.

— s·e·v·e·n·t·e·e·n —

The following day was a blur, as Lily barely paid attention in classes, anxious to sneak out and head to the basement. Not because she necessarily *wanted* to, but because they needed to cross it off their list. And there *had* to be an entrance *somewhere*.

Having had her grades follow her to McMillan, and catching up to the current units the students here were on, Lily was on track to move to eleventh grade with Caroline and the others in the fall. No homework to keep her busy made the day drag, and made her a bit restless. She noticed the seniors were restless in general, all excited to be almost done with school for good. Lily thought the school would seem empty without them, even though she'd only interacted with them in the lounge and cafeteria.

While they waited for Tommy to give the all clear after curfew had been called, Caroline told Lily not all the seniors would be graduating at the end of June.

"There are a handful who will still be here for the first half of next year and then graduating in December. It all depends on when they came to the school. What year, when during the year, and how they did on their placement tests." Caroline ticked items off on her fingers and then lowered her voice to mimic Mr. Erne. "Dad says *it's still a school and we still have standards and regulations to meet.*"

Lily wondered which students were staying but didn't ask. She silently hoped Alyssa was graduating.

"Next spring will be the first time since me and Dad have been here when there won't be any seniors, only juniors—unless they bring some in, or some sophomores. New kids."

"And that's not normal?"

"It's happened before, but not since I've been here."

Tommy popped through the door from the hall. "All clear."

Lily jumped, not expecting him, and promptly forgot what they had been talking about. Instead, she felt the anxiety about the basement immediately creep up her throat like her body was threatening to vomit.

"Let's go." Caroline stood and put her sneakers on. They'd been running around barefoot or in socks after hours until now and Lily cocked her head at her roommate. Caroline cringed. "The basement floor is filthy *and* freezing. You'll want shoes. But pick soft ones that will be quiet in the hall."

Lily nodded and grabbed her flip-flops, but remembered the strange flapping noise they made, and swapped them out for the pair she'd gotten for gym class. Shoes on, she pulled her hair back into a ponytail and took a deep breath.

Sneaking out of their room had gotten easy. Moving quickly and quietly to the back stairs was almost second nature. And gently descending without noise had become an award-worthy skill of stealth.

Continuing down past the first floor they came to a large, fairly clean, cement basement with high walls made of oversized bricks. The floor was a slate gray, and Lily couldn't tell if it was the natural color of the cement or if it was painted, until she saw spots where previous chips had been painted over. A closer inspection showed *several* layers of paint covered the floor. The walls had once been painted a clean white, which had grayed with age to become the color of dust on paper. Cracks and discoloration in the lines of mortar showed the true age of the basement, and belied to the false sense of sterility. It was neither the walls nor floor, which gave Lily pause.

Directly in front of them, ten feet from the bottom of the stairs, was a wall of wire fencing with a closed gate in the center of it. Tommy walked through it and stopped, waiting for them on the other side. Lily wasn't surprised by his boldness. Tommy had always been braver than she was, in *every* situation.

Beyond the gate and past Tommy, Lily could see bits of forgotten black pebbles and dust on the floor next to an old wooden door up high on the wall and knew it was an abandoned coal shoot. Further back, the wall of an enclosed room jutted out into the center and turned away from them. Above it, pipes of all sizes ran every direction and she imagined the room itself was where the water heater and filters and other such things were kept. On the right side of the expanse, Lily could see two doors, one had a warning sign posted on the front but she couldn't make out the words, just the symbols. The basement continued into the darkness beyond the two rooms, but Lily couldn't be sure how far from her vantage point. Between her and the answer was a closed gate.

"Caroline?" Lily raised her eyebrows, as she heard what she thought was a young girl. The tickle in her ears told her it was a ghost. She looked at Tommy while waiting for Caroline's response, but he didn't seem to notice it.

"What?" Caroline looked at Lily.

"Um…" Lily's eyes danced around the area as she listened.

"This? This has always been here. I knew it was here. But it's never locked. It's just for show." Caroline headed straight for the gate on the fence and stopped abruptly. "Well, it's not *supposed* to be locked."

Lily could see a new looking padlock holding the gate to the fence. She heard a light clank as Caroline tested the lock, followed by a *harrumph* sound, reminding her of when Papa disagreed with something he saw on television. The tickle and voice seemed to fade and Caroline hadn't noticed it, so Lily said nothing.

"We'll just have to go the other way. They can't lock that one, it would block the headmaster." Caroline turned back and headed past Lily toward the stairs.

Lily followed Tommy and Caroline back up one flight, past the classrooms, across the wide hall in front of the office, cafeteria, and nurses station, before finally turning into the West Wing classroom corridor. Lily didn't know if she'd expected it to be different or not, but it wasn't. It was a mirror image of their classrooms and while Lily wanted to peek inside the little glass windows on each door, she had to keep up as Caroline hurried toward the back stairs.

Back down to the gray and dust-colored basement, they were met by another wall of wire with a closed gate. This one, true to Caroline's word, was unlocked and they opened it slowly to avoid making noise.

Along the outer wall on this side of the basement were several doors marked with brass numbers, like the one Lily had seen on Mr. Erne's suite.

Caroline saw Lily looking at the doors and waved their direction. "Storage lockers for the teachers. The tunnel for the headmaster's cottage is behind the door with no number on it. And over here, canned goods to last an apocalypse." She looked to the right and Lily followed her gaze to find rows and rows of shelves lined with every type of canned food she could imagine—fruits, veggies, meats, pasta, even pudding was visible in the dim flickering of the hanging fluorescents.

Caroline pointed forward to the wall in front of them. She put a finger to her mouth to tell Lily to be quiet. "That is the janitor's apartment. The door is around the corner. I've never seen him out after curfew, but let's be super quiet anyway."

Lily nodded, remembering the man with the charcoal rubbed across his fingers and thoughts of dead girls in his head.

They turned at the wall and stepped into a large open area. Two small restrooms, clearly marked for gender, were on the left next to the laundry room doors. To the right, toward the front of the building, was a set of stairs going up. Lily's internal compass led her to believe the stairs led to the front door. In front of them, before the hallway turned into the portion of the basement she'd seen from the other gate, was a large walled off room marked BOILER.

Hmmm, is the boiler separate from the water?

Lily thought of the other room with all the pipes above it. She turned to ask Caroline and found the girl inspecting the walls outside the laundry room. As Lily watched, Caroline crossed and lightly tapped along the housing for the small stairs leading to the main floor by the front door. The entire time, she kept her eye on the door to her right—the janitor's apartment.

Caroline shook her head at Lily and motioned they go in the laundry room. Lily pulled open the heavy door and walked into the bright light of machines and tables. She waited for Caroline to pull the door shut behind her.

"Why didn't we just come down through the kitchen? Or even the main steps by the front door? Why risk the back steps? And the *West Wing?*" Lily furrowed her brows at Caroline.

"Where's the adventure in that?" Caroline smiled at Tommy and he snickered.

Lily knew she wasn't brave, but she was here now, in a basement of all places, and had to try and pretend. "Well okay then, where are we looking?"

"I checked the exterior of the room and over

by the stairs just in case. But I guess it would be in here somewhere if anywhere, right?"

Lily shrugged and moved to the left of the door. She began methodically pushing, touching and inspecting the areas of the wall behind the tables and machines.

"Tommy," she whispered back to him, seeing him following Caroline along the opposite wall.

He turned and rushed over to her.

"See if you can go through these walls. See if there's gaps like you found upstairs."

"Okay." He walked straight through the wall next to Lily and came back spattering imaginary debris. "Nothing but dirt and worms."

"Over here?" Caroline called and he crossed to her side and repeated the process.

He appeared again several feet away from Caroline, and Lily felt hope flush her face, but he shook his head. "Dirt."

"What about in the closed rooms? The utility rooms?" Lily looked toward the door. "They're dangerous and locked from us, but you can check in those, right?"

He nodded and went *through* the doors to the open portion of the basement, the girls following but having to open and close the doors as they did. They watched as he went into and back out of each of the rooms, even daring to go peek in the janitor's apartment. He returned with a shudder.

"He's a *big* scary guy, isn't he?"

It was Lily's turn to nod.

"See, Caroline, I told you there wasn't nothing down here." Tommy put his hands on his hips.

"Wait, you told her? When?" Lily looked between the two with confusion.

Caroline's gaze dropped down to her feet for a moment, then back up at Lily and spoke with a weak smile and soft voice. "Adventure?"

"Caroline!" Lily whispered hoarsely, wanting to scold her but afraid to wake the janitor. "Let's get out of here."

Caroline turned back toward the West Wing stairs and Lily shushed loudly to get her attention. She pointed to the main stairs. Caroline shook her head and motioned for Lily to follow. "I want to check the tunnel."

"The tunnel?"

Tommy followed Caroline without question and Lily was forced to go along with it. Under the stairs, which led back up to the first floor, an opening in the wall had been retrofitted with the addition of a wooden jamb and door. Caroline opened it and Lily looked past her to peer inside.

"Hmmm, it's dark." Lily said, imagining that would mean they were done.

"I know." Caroline pulled a small flashlight from her back pocket, and Lily knew she'd planned to go in there the whole time. "Come on."

Tommy squinted into the darkness and shook his head. "No way." He promptly sat on the steps.

Lily turned and stared at Tommy for a moment. Tommy the brave, the one who would go into anywhere and check anything, was sitting this one out? *Why?* Lily was now *more* worried about the tunnel, but hesitantly followed Caroline and the tiny cone of light. The faster she went along with Caroline's wishes, the faster they could get out of there and back upstairs.

The tunnel smelled old and wet with a natural putridness to it, as if the cement walls were sweating and earth was used to wipe them down. Caroline poked at a couple spots, but seemed less concerned about finding the hidden door than with just getting through the tunnel.

At the other end, they found a closed door. Not put in as an afterthought like at the other end, but rather a heavy metal door as old as the foundation of the PE building they were below. It didn't budge and was obviously locked from the other side.

"Oh well. It was worth a try."

"What was?" Lily was confused. There was no way the entrance to the passage in the walls was down this dark tunnel.

"I always wanted to go through here, to see

what was inside, but I don't like basements and didn't want to go alone." Caroline smiled at Lily with a slightly pained expression. "Thanks for coming along."

What?

Lily would *never* have gone in the basement if *that's* what this was all about. *Never*. She hated them. She was afraid of them. And there were people in this one—both living and dead. If it wouldn't have alerted the janitor, she would have yelled at Caroline. Instead, she grabbed the flashlight from her roommate, turned, and started walking back to the main building.

A noise in front of them startled the girls and they both stopped. Lily's heart skipped a beat before Tommy appeared in the beam of light.

"I don't like being down here anymore. Can we go upstairs now?"

"Yes, yes we can, Tommy." Lily whispered and shot Caroline a side-glance. When it was safe to speak, she was going to let her know she didn't like this.

Wanting out as fast as possible, but trying to avoid the West Wing, they crossed over to the main stairs by the front door and headed up. As they came out onto the first floor, prepared to turn and go directly up to the second and their bedrooms, a voice stopped them.

"What exactly are you two doing up at this hour?"

Lily was so startled she was afraid her bladder would give way, and she heard Caroline gasp in front of her. Turning, she saw a young teacher with short shaggy purple-dyed hair and a hand on her hip, standing outside the cafeteria. The blue of her eyes was striking and Lily could clearly see them in the light of the main hall.

The woman's thoughts were jittery and loud. They flitted around disjointedly in an angry staccato. *Long blonde ponytail looks like Mom's when she burned it down. When she burned* him. *He needed it. Earned it. Hope* you're *burning now, Mom. Teens with talents? They know nothing of talent here. The things I did as a teen, the things I got away with. I've killed more people than pets, and they were all so very concerned about the pets.*

Lily couldn't follow the out-of-context thoughts from mother to burning to pets, but she could feel the wanton violence. The woman was thinking about death and killing, and she wasn't afraid. She wasn't mourning. She was yearning.

And it scared Lily.

"Sorry, just going up and down the stairs a few times to tire ourselves out. Got talking about ghosts and scared ourselves silly. Couldn't sleep. We're heading back up." Caroline went straight up the stairs without another word or approval from the teacher, and Lily hurried to follow.

At the top of the stairs, Caroline turned back with wide eyes and exhaled relief when they weren't followed. "I can't believe that worked."

"Who in the hell was *that*?"

Caroline blinked at Lily's use of vulgarity. "I— I don't know. One of the teachers from the other side. Grace *something,* I think. Why?"

"She scares the crap out of me. She's killed people."

"Yeah... that's probably why she's on the other side." Caroline turned and continued toward their bedroom. Lily followed, watching the West Wing until she rounded the corner and it was out of sight.

"No more games. No more wild goose chases."
Lily looked at Caroline as sternly as she could
muster. Tommy's snicker meant her expression
wasn't convincing.

"Okay, okay, I'm sorry. I won't do it again."
Caroline held her hands up in front of her. "I'm
not even suggesting we wait until after curfew.
With Mr. Williamson sick today, it's a free period
right now, and no one is doing homework in the
library. Everyone's either in their room or the
lounge, so let's go look there again. It has to be
in there."

"What about the laundry hall?" The pitch in
Lily's voice rose with insistence. "I want to show
you something in there by the elevator."

"We can check that first if you *want*. Sure.
But let's go. We have less than an hour."

Tommy looked at Lily, his eyes imploring
her. "There's someone hiding, Lily. We should
find them. We should help them."

"And why don't we just tell your dad,

Caroline? Why not tell the teachers? Or the dean?"

"Because we sound crazy. *A ghost saw a passageway with stuff in it.*" Caroline raised one eyebrow. "Crazy. First we get proof, then we tell my dad."

Lily hemmed and hawed, but understood the idea of people calling her crazy more than Caroline could know. "Fair enough. Let's go."

Just past the library was a narrow hallway that traveled the entire depth of the building along the library. Along the left side were shelves, closets, and cupboards of linens and various school supplies. At the end, was the elevator, which led to the kitchen and then the laundry room below. It also went up, where the non-teaching staff suites were located.

On the left side, after the storage and shelving, there was a small cubby with a narrow laundry cart tucked into it. Draped over the side, as well as folded on the shelf above it, were laundry bags.

"This is what I was talking 'bout." Lily pulled the cart out, and stepped into the spot it had been. "This indent ain't as deep as the cupboards. Open that one there and reach inside, how far does your arm go?"

Caroline crinkled her eyebrows at Lily, but followed the directions. "If I put my hand on the back wall, I have to reach in pretty far. Probably six inches longer than my arm?"

Lily stepped out of the cart area and reached back into it, her hand resting against the wall. "It's not as far here. The wall doesn't go back as far. The wall where you are is closer to the outside brick than right here."

"So is the entrance in there?" Caroline pulled her arm out and walked down to Lily, ducking to look around the area.

Lily shrugged. "Tommy, am I right? Is there a gap in here?"

Tommy ducked and walked into the wall. He walked back out and nodded at them. "That is absolutely part of the walkway. I'm telling ya, it goes all the way around the library."

The two of them pushed, poked and knocked on every bit of the wall in the cubby. Starting opposite each other and working past the other, they went across the area twice.

"There's nothing here." Caroline sounded exasperated.

"But you see what I mean, right?" Lily pointed to the wall.

Caroline nodded. "I do. Maybe it starts in the library and comes back around to land here."

"Maybe."

Tommy walked through the opposite wall, into the library. He came out again by the entrance of the narrow linen hall. "And it goes all along here on this side, too."

The girls eyed at each other for a moment. Caroline pushed the cart back in and Lily led the way back to the library.

"It's got to be in here, right?" Lily considered the edge of the walls, nearly every inch covered with shelves of books.

Except the computer lab.

"What about back there?" Caroline pointed to the back corner. "Does it go past the computer lab?"

Tommy nodded and moved his finger as he spoke. "From the right edge over there, all the way down, across the back, over to the linen wall, and up this wall too. From above it would look like an E with half the bottom line missing. 'Cos I can't read too good, but I know my letters." He beamed.

"Lily," Caroline turned to her slowly, her brows knit together in deep thought.

"Yeah?"

"Where'd you see the ghost girl?"

"That was over here." Lily walked through the room toward the librarian desk. Standing to the side of it, she pointed to the small office without a door on the side. "Both times I seen her, she came an' went from back there. CJ saw her though, so it wasn't a ghost. A West Winger snooping where she shouldn't?"

"Maybe. What'd she look like? I know a couple of them. Not all, but some."

"She's got short strawberry blonde hair, like a pixie cut, and I think her eyes were blue. She's pretty, but *fierce* looking. And kinda tall."

"Lily, that's the girl." Tommy whispered.

"What girl, Tommy?"

"The one what was holding me in the hall that night. The one what said *don't move* and then I couldn't. That's what *she* looked like."

"Caroline?" Lily turned to her roommate and saw the girl's color had washed from her face.

"Jezzy. You just described Jezzy." Caroline's eyes danced back and forth focusing on nothing as Lily watched her friend's mind reel. "She's not gone. Was *never* gone. She's still here. And she's loose in the walls? We need to tell someone!"

A loud clicking noise from the small office caused them all to turn toward it. A small panel was popped out away from the wall, hanging open on small hinges. Jezzy had climbed halfway out—one leg still in the darkness of the passageway behind her—when she froze and turned to meet their gaze.

"You won't tell anyone." Jezzy spoke clearly and calmly, and continued to climb free of the wall.

Lily stared at the girl. *Really? You think we'll just*—

Peripherally, Lily could see Caroline's head slowly nod up and down. Tommy had frozen in place. But Lily was fine. She had free will and a strong desire to find Mr. Erne.

Lily's mouth dropped in awe as she realized she was immune to the girl's powers for some reason. She could hear her just fine. And she could see the anger and desperation and intent in the girl's expression. She *knew* she should have been commanded as easily as Caroline and Tommy had been, but she wasn't, and she didn't know why.

Jezzy cocked her head and squinted at her. "You. Won't. Tell." She spoke each word on its own, punctuating the idea she was trying to force into Lily's mind.

Lily raised her eyebrows and concentrated for a moment. Nothin'. She couldn't hear the girl's thoughts. It was as blocked as Caroline's.

Oh Lord, can she read mine? Does she know *she's not affecting me?*

The grandfather clock began to strike, and both Jezzy and Lily jumped. Caroline did not. And Jezzy flashed a look of confusion and disbelief at Lily.

"Who are you? *What* are you?" Jezzy spoke with hatred and fear.

Oh Lord, she knows.

The clock continued to strike. Even in it's muted state, the chimes were loud enough to cover Lily's jagged breath, pounding heart, and whatever it was Jezzy was ordering Lily to do.

Jezzy's eyes went wide. She jumped up and

slid across the desk to get past Lily, knocking papers, pens, books and the nameplate to the floor as she did so. The final chime rang out as the library door closed and a stunned Lily turned to Caroline to find her friend still frozen in place.

Lily grabbed Caroline's shoulders and shook her friend as hard as she dared.

"Caroline! Wake up!"

Caroline blinked several times at Lily. "Oh my god, Jezzy! We can't tell anyone!"

"Yes we can! She told you *not* to. Ignore that. Listen to *me*. We're gonna tell right now. Come on."

"Was *that* the third voice you heard, Lily? Was it her all along?"

Lily studied Caroline and wondered why she chose now to ask, then realized she was still under Jezzy's directive. "No, Caroline. I wasn't hearing a *living* voice. They tickle my ears funny. I can tell the difference. And um... I can't hear anything at all coming from Jezzy." She swallowed hard. The silence in Jezzy scared Lily like no other silence.

Lily turned toward Tommy.

She couldn't shake him. She couldn't touch him. She yelled and screamed his name. She snapped her fingers in his face. She clapped her hands hard in his ear. And Tommy shook his head and finally focused on her.

"Come on, Tommy. We have to stop her."

He looked at her with a furrowed brow and shook his head.

"She told you not to. Ignore it. Both of you ignore it!" Lily glanced around the room in a panic and then back to them. "Okay, we're *not* going to tell, but we're going to find her, follow her, so we know where she is. Okay?"

Maybe that would work.

"Okay." Tommy nodded.

"Let's hurry, before we lose her." Caroline was on board.

Lily sighed and rushed for the door. As they pulled the library door open, they heard the first scream. Running toward the commotion, they headed to the stairs.

Several students were coming up and trying to get past Jezzy, who appeared to be *trying* to go down. *Toward an exit, I expect,* Lily thought, trying to figure out where Jezzy was going.

Jezzy grunted and growled at the flowing mob of teens for several moments, then stopped pushing and took a step back. Jezzy pointed in front of her and spoke as calmly as she had to Lily in the library. "Jump."

Lily watched in horror as CJ hopped over the railing of the second floor staircase and dropped,

· 190 ·

the girl's eyes wide with disbelief and fear. The commotion in the stairwell grew louder.

— t · w · e · n · t · y —

The following chorus of screams came from students at the top, as well as the bottom, of the stairs. Jezzy fought the flow of the crowd, as they pushed in panic to get past her and find the safety of their rooms. She turned back toward the library and sprinted for the East Wing dorms.

Lily and Caroline ran after her, as Lily tried to figure out what to do if they caught her.

Jezzy ran past doors as they opened, students poking their heads out and stepping into the hallway. Lily saw them all reacting to whatever she was saying as she passed them.

A blonde girl, a senior Lily hadn't properly met yet, turned and banged her head against the wall hard enough to immediately drop to the ground.

Kals suddenly began flailing her arms in all directions and ran to attack Odette.

Lily's eyes widened as she watched Alyssa's cheeks puff out while she held her breath in an exaggerated manner, like a toddler having a tantrum.

Miko stepped out into the hall, immediately raised her red glasses and squinted toward Lily. Miko smiled at Tommy, and then jumped as screams from the main stairwell rang back through the vastness of the building toward them. She turned toward the commotion, her gaze following the girl running down the hall. Miko put her glasses back on and stood up straight. "Nope, not a ghost. What the—"

"It's Jezzy!" Caroline called back, as she and Lily gave chase.

"Come with me, Miko." Tommy called and she moved her glasses to the top of her head, tucked into her hair. "We've got to get help." Tommy ran the opposite direction of Lily and Miko followed.

Lily realized Jezzy's commands had worn off Tommy and wondered how long Caroline would be held to them. She turned back and continued her pursuit of Jezzy, Caroline at her side, and worry crawling up into her heart and mind.

I finally find somewhere I'm accepted and someone is hurting all my new friends? They're hurt. They're bleeding. They could die if I don't stop her.

Lily spurred forward, almost falling down the stairs as she chased Jezzy to the first floor. Lily half-wished the girl had tried the basement, knowing that escape route was blocked by a shiny new padlock.

Running by the classroom doors, Lily saw teachers and students alike looking on in horror. Lily could tell some of them recognized Jezzy. Lily couldn't hear what the other girl was saying, but she could see the affects, just as she had upstairs. Two senior boys began fighting. Another started hitting himself in the head with his schoolbook. And Mr. Williamson pushed a female student back so hard she fell to her bottom.

At the end of the hall they turned, and Lily watched Miss Mac step out from her desk only to suddenly freeze. Her lips quivered and her eyes were full of fear. Miz Yost ran into her office and shut the door. Jezzy turned toward the front door, no adults trying to stop her.

Lily and Caroline pivoted to face the front door as it burst open. The gardener, *Warren,* rushed into the chaos in time to meet the dean descending the final few steps. On the floor in front of the dean lay CJ, the blood pool around her short dark hair had spread to the tile grout in the floor and was slowly traveling along its lines. Tasha kneeled next to her, her hands splayed across the fallen girl's chest in what Lily knew was an attempt to calm CJ. As Tasha turned to Jezzy with hatred in her eyes, she met Lily's gaze and shook her head. Lily swallowed hard as she understood the message and watched tears fall down Tasha's face.

"Jezebel Babak, you will stop this right now!" Dean Duran barked at Jezzy and the girl skidded to a stop. She screamed something back that Lily didn't quite catch.

The dean stared at Jezzy, and Jezzy stared back. Lily watched the standoff, wondering what abilities the dean had that no one knew about.

How is she holding Jezzy so still?

Sam cried out from the stairwell and rushed toward his sister's body, brushing past the dean on his way. Miko and Tommy were right behind him.

As they reached the bottom step, Miko skidded to a halt and stared at CJ in horror. Tears instantly welled in her eyes, as her hand flew up to cover her mouth.

Lily watched as Tommy ignored the body, his gaze flitting between Jezzy and Lily.

"Jezzy's powers don't work on me." Lily whispered to Caroline.

"What?"

"Back in the library, her words didn't work. And I can't hear her *inner* voice at all. That's why she looked scared when I thought she was a ghost, 'cos she was trying to command me and it weren't working. That's why she ran."

"So?"

"So I can stop her…" Lily took a step forward. She didn't want anyone else hurt. She could hear Sam's pain screaming across the hall. She could hear the fear of her other classmates, running up the stairs and cowering in shadows. Lily's anger began to rage inside her, and all the voices around her—both inside and out—began talking and shouting over each other in a cacophony of confusion.

I can stop this. Lily started to walk with purpose, heading directly for Jezzy.

I won't let you hurt any more friends.

Lily saw Tommy hold up his hand and shake his head at her. The sadness in his eyes contradicted the bravery of his stance. "I'll stop her."

"What? No." Lily felt her heart sink as Tommy ran straight at Jezzy and disappeared.

Lily ran forward, almost tripping over her own feet in shock as Tommy vanished. She spun Jezzy around, prepared to do whatever necessary to stop the girl. But Jezzy didn't fight her. She didn't move against Lily at all. Instead, Jezzy stared at Lily with utter fear in her eyes.

Lily watched as Jezzy began to twitch and twist, screaming and raging and yelling at nothing.

"Get out! Get out, get out, get out!" Jezzy's body contorted, as she doubled over.

She groaned, as she stood back up, her movements jerky and violent against nothing but herself. Jezzy flailed her arms and kicked her legs out. She turned in a tight circle and looked like she was trying to avoid an angry hornet.

"No! Get him out! Get him out!"

Jezzy's mouth fell slack and she dropped to her knees. Tears of distress began to run down her face. Her lip started to quiver, and she glared up at Lily, eyes wide with fear and resistance.

And then a softness that wasn't Jezzy washed across her expression.

Jezzy's eyes were streams of tears and she was shaking as if trying to move against restraints but was unable. Suddenly, she moved in a jerky fashion, a puppet responding to invisible strings, and raised her hands out in front of her.

Jezzy looked at the groundskeeper and spoke in the voice of a little boy. "Now."

Warren sprinted forward, stepping past Lily to push Jezzy to the ground and straddle her. He put a hand over her mouth, preventing her from giving orders, and pinned her arms at her side.

"I have tape!" The janitor came from somewhere behind Lily with a roll of duct tape, a strip already torn free and held out in front of him.

Miz Yost appeared from her office and joined the effort, kneeling next to CJ. She had a cell phone in her hand, and was already talking to emergency medical personnel on the other end of the call.

Miss Mac suddenly broke from her frozen state next to Caroline, and Lily watched as the woman cried out and rushed toward Sam and gripped his shoulders. Sam yanked from Miss Mac and fell across CJ's broken body. He mumbled incoherent promises and regrets, as he sobbed uncontrollably. Miss Mac grabbed him and pulled him away from CJ. She wrapped him in her arms, holding him as tight as if he were her own and shielding his face against her chest. She cooed softly as she began to rock. Tears of her own fell, as she gawked in horror at CJ's still form. Muffled by Miss Mac's shoulder, Sam continued to blubber and ramble, his breaths coming in deep jagged gasps.

Jezzy began to wiggle again, her head swinging side to side, and Lily knew Tommy had lost control of her. She turned violently toward Lily and hissed through the tape on her mouth. Wild hatred changed the flow of tears running down Jezzy's cheeks.

Lily backed up and panic flooded into her chest, tightening her throat. She looked around at the faces and registered each one, but didn't find the one she sought.

"Tommy?" She began moving around and through the milling students, each of them reacting in their own way. Some cried, some held each other, and others cowered. All of them upset.

All the inside anguish screamed so very loudly.

Lily frantically tried to block out the turmoil around her—the crushing, overbearing distress coming from everyone all at once. She tried to block the voices of the living, all of them—both spoken or simply thought—and frantically looked around for a small red shirt.

A familiar shirt. A torn shirt.

QUIET! She screamed mentally at everyone around her, as she feared the worst.

And it went quiet inside. Deathly quiet. She had *made* it all quiet. All of it. All of them. All their pain and fear, their anguish and cries. All their inner voices were held at bay and their outside voices seemed dampened, as if she were in the bath, sunk below the water.

And in the silence she tried again to find him.

"Tommy?" Her whisper cracked and her jaw clenched. "Tommy…"

When her words didn't work, she used her inner voice and pleaded with the boy to show himself. *Tommy. Please, Tommy…*

Lily walked through the chaos twice before she slumped to the stairs, landing on the second step in a broken heap of heartache. She looked between CJ's unmoving body and Jezzy's restrained one. She studied Jezzy's eyes, searching for him inside. Tommy wasn't there. Not anymore.

Tommy wasn't anywhere.

She couldn't find him. She couldn't hear him. She couldn't *feel* him.

Lily's stomach became a hollow pit, as bile

rose in her throat. She swallowed it back and felt the heat rise in her eyes as tears welled. Deep inside she realized there was an emptiness to her surroundings she had never felt before.

And she knew.

She knew he didn't make it.

He wasn't strong enough.

Tommy had sacrificed himself for her. For Caroline and Miko. For the rest of them. As the chaos of voices and thoughts broke through her shock, as the sirens blared ever closer in the distance, the world became really loud in his absence.

For the first time in a long time, Lily was alone.

— about the author —

Kelli Owen is the author of more than a dozen books, including TEETH, FLOATERS, and WAITING OUT WINTER. Her fiction spans the genres from thrillers to psychological horror, with an occasional bloodbath, and an even rarer happy ending. She has attended countless writing conventions, participated on dozens of panels, and spoken at the CIA Headquarters in Langley, VA regarding both her writing and the field in general. Born and raised in Wisconsin, she now lives in Destination, Pennsylvania. Visit her website at kelliowen.com for more information. F/F

— author note —

Frank Errington was a lovely, wonderful, kind, smart, funny, amazing human who unfortunately didn't live to see this finished. As a reviewer and a friend, I had used his name previously (as I tend to do) in DECEIVER, but only as a passing *body* in a story. At a get together earlier this year, I told him about his new and improved appearance (hidden in here behind his father's name with his mother's surname as we agreed upon). The world lost his smile and gentle laugh, but he left behind many *many* friends, both authors and fellow reviewers alike, and a well known, far-spread love of the genre. To that, I humbly add a character who will stand in that shadow and carry on for several books in this series. Rest well, Frank, you will be missed. May 31, 2019.

See how Lily May's story started...

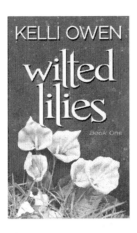

It's not that Lily May Holloway is a broken,
battered teenager recently escaped
from her kidnapper.

It's not that she may or may not have
killed him to escape.

The question on Detective Travis Butler's mind
is—what exactly does the death of little
Tommy Jenkins have to do with her
kidnapper?

And why does the man behind the one-way
glass want the detective to entertain
Lily's tales of speaking to the dead... and
being able to hear the thoughts of the living?

Made in the USA
Middletown, DE
21 July 2019